Dr Sutcliffe asked Sarah to wait in one of the armchairs around the lounge area while he went into a room at the end. Sarah saw a white-coated man coming back with him. His shoulders were well back, and his dark head held high.

Her hand was grasped by cool, strong fingers. 'Hello,' he said quietly. 'I'm Neil Patterson.'

She saw the concern in his dark eyes as she searched his face for news which she was inwardly dreading to be told. The room misted slightly and she swayed. 'I'm sorry. . .' Her voice still seemed too faint, but as composure returned she knew that she could cope now.

'No apologies needed,' he said quietly. 'I just wish I had better news for you. I didn't imagine you would get here so quickly. Dr Sutcliffe tells me you're a professional nurse, which greatly relieves the situation for me, though not for you. Because naturally you will want to know the exact nature of your father's injuries.'

He came nearer and put his hand on her shoulder. 'I wish I could wrap this up a little, Nurse Hillier, but you know there is no way I can do that, don't you?'

Elizabeth Petty lives in a cottage on the outskirts of Southampton with her husband, now retired. She has two married daughters and four teenage grandchildren, of whom she is very proud.

She began her writing career over twenty years ago by having short stories and serials published, many of which were translated into foreign languages, but after writing her first Medical Romance she felt this was her metier. She feels strongly that there is a depth and reality in these books with which readers can identify, many of them having experienced some of the traumas themselves, as well as the great care and support of the medical profession as a whole. *Calling Nurse Hillier* is her ninth book in this genre.

Previous Title

THE BEST MEDICINE

CALLING NURSE HILLIER

BY

ELIZABETH PETTY

MILLS & BOON LIMITED
ETON HOUSE   18–24 PARADISE ROAD
RICHMOND   SURREY   TW9 1SR

First published in Great Britain 1991 by Mills & Boon Limited

© *Elizabeth Petty 1991*

Australian copyright 1991

ISBN 0 263 12869 5

Set in 10 on 10½ pt Linotron Times 15-9104-59991 Typeset in Great Britain by Centracet, Cambridge Made and printed in Great Britain

CHAPTER ONE

SARAH HILLIER drew back the pale yellow and grey curtains from around the bed of one of her post-operative patients and smiled reassuringly as she said softly, 'Try to get some sleep now.' The man in the bed returned her smile, if somewhat weakly; but it was a smile, and the first one since his surgery.

Just then, Sister-in-charge walked briskly into the ward, her buxom figure in the navy dress bobbing up and down, as did the frilled cap on her neat grey hair.

'Can we have a word, Staff? A few changes in our schedule, I'm afraid. I have to go to a meeting and then after an early lunch take Sister Reeves's lecture for her. She thinks she's coming down with influenza. Are you up to time?'

'Almost, Sister.'

'Well, come into the office and I'll go through a few things with you.'

Sarah followed her senior, noticing that two nurses were preparing a post-operative bed ready for Mr Barker on his return from theatre where he was undergoing emergency surgery. There had been a flap on earlier which had meant calling in a senior consult-ant; this was nothing unusual and Sarah coped well with emergencies. She had been well trained and liked working with Sister Maine on men's surgical. Now, it seemed, she was to have more responsibility, as Sister outlined the amended afternoon schedule.

'I think that's all, Staff. I'll be back around four, I hope.'

'Right. I'd better go to it, then.'

Sarah got up from the chair opposite Sister's desk and straightened the grey-checked cotton dress, the purple belt with its silver buckle, of which she was justly proud; accentuating her waist Sister was too as she watched her go back to her work, the golden brown hair pinned neatly at the back of a well-shaped head under the tiny cap. She had had quite a lot to do with the blossoming of that particular girl, having been at St David's for most of her working life and watched Sarah's progress with more than just a professional interest.

She and Sarah's mother had been at school together and when Mrs Hillier, years later, became a patient on her ward suffering from leukaemia, from which she subsequently died, she got to know twelve-year-old Sarah and her father very well. Her mother would have been proud of her, she thought now as she put her sheaf of papers in the drawer and closed her office door. Because I am.

When Sarah drove out through the hospital gates on that late-April evening, she looked across at the blue Mendip Hills with their dark shadows and mysterious beauty, the softly rolling hills. She loved this part of England, especially in spring. And wondered how her father was enjoying his stay in Canada. He had flown to Vancouver for a pharmaceutical conference and, apart from one phone call, she hadn't heard from him since.

Turning into the driveway of the house they both knew as home, she sighed thankfully at the thought of an evening with supper on a tray, her bare feet up, a comfortable armchair, soft music and her current nursing magazine, and an early night.

Opening the front door, she bent to pick up the mail on the carpet and a post-card from Canada of high mountains reflected in the clear water of a lake, trees growing up the mountain sides and yellow flowers along the shores and above, a dazzlingly blue sky and not a cloud in sight.

Looks good, she thought, as she read what was on

the back. 'This is Jasper—in the Rockies. I'm here for the weekend. Back to Vancouver tomorrow. Colder than I expected. Lots of snow still around. Be home next week. Dad.'

Well—it would be cold if there's snow around, she mused. It will be good to have him back. Switching on the kettle for coffee and taking out eggs for a mushroom omelette, she concentrated on her meal.

Not that they lived in each other's pockets. She and her father had their own sets of friends. No special man though—not since Jeremy. She had been over the moon about that young doctor, until he had accused her of reading more into that particular relationship than he'd intended. She certainly had, and he had done nothing to disillusion her either. She had been so blind. So stupid. But it would not happen again, she'd decided. And it hadn't. He had left the hospital soon afterwards; was it really a year ago? And why had she thought of him specially tonight? The bowl of spring flowers on the table in the hall perhaps had triggered off her memory towards him.

Much later in the evening, when the telephone rang in the hall, she was immersed in an article on new methods of intravenous therapy; she reluctantly put this down to go and answer the phone and was surprised to hear a female voice with a strong Canadian accent asking if that was the Hillier residence.

'I'm calling Miss Sarah Hillier.'

'Hello. Yes—I'm here. Who is that?'

'Please hold—I have Dr Patterson for you.'

Her heart missed a beat. She had expected to hear her father's voice, instead of which a man's deeper slower drawl was asking if she were alone.

'Yes, I am. Is something wrong?' It was what Sister asked relatives of patients if she were the bearer of bad news. He hesitated before answering, obviously deciding to come straight out with it.

'Miss Hillier. I have to tell you that your father was

in a car accident today. He sustained serious injuries, I'm afraid.'

Her heart seemed to be in her throat.

'How serious, Dr Patterson?'

'There are multiple injuries and he is, of course, in intensive care. I am sorry to have to tell you this, Miss Hillier, but from your father's diary it would seem that you are his next of kin and I think you should fly over here as soon as possible. You could probably get an emergency seat on Air Canada if you call them now.'

Sarah's hands were shaking so that she could barely hold the receiver. Her brain was insisting that this could not be true, his masculine voice the only sure thing as he said strongly, 'Are you still there, Miss Hillier?'

'Yes.'

'Are you OK?'

'Yes—I—I'll get on to them right away.'

'Good. You will need to take a yellow cab from the airport and come straight here—to the main hospital; ask for me. Neil Patterson. I'm so sorry to have to tell you this.'

'Thank you. . .' she whispered as she replaced the receiver.

Her voice broke; she pressed her hand to her mouth. No time for this: she must phone Heathrow, get on a flight to Vancouver—somehow.

She phoned Heathrow and Air Canada bookings. They promised to ring her back within the hour. This just was not happening. But it was and she needed air—lots of it—and went to open the door into the garden. Cold air on her face and drawn into her lungs in deep gulps helped a lot while all the time her brain kept repeating, it can't be happening. . .her father's card—it was like a nightmare. But doctors didn't create nightmares and from this one she knew she wouldn't wake up.

The sound of a car next door invaded her consciousness. Normal sounds, except that nothing would ever be the same again. She called to them through the darkness.

'Oh, please help me, Mr Beales. Please come in— something dreadful has happened.'

They saw her standing there, still in shock, and came at once. It was they who phoned Sister Maine and ten minutes later her car drew up in the driveway. She came into the house, an unfamiliar figure in yellow trousers and a navy blue sweater who took over completely and even stayed the night, sitting with Sarah through the long-drawn-out hours. But, her flight arranged, Mr Beales was coming in at seven o'clock to drive her to the airport and there was still a lot to do. She heard Mrs Beales say something about seeing to the fridge and closing the house but it didn't seem important at the time. It was as if she were in a vacuum, making the motions but nothing registering very much as she packed a case with clothes in which she had no interest, but just hoped they were right for Canada.

And not until the plane was taxiing down the tarmac, hesitating before that final burst of speed until it became airborne, did Sarah finally give in and accept the reason for being on that plane as she lay back and closed her eyes, her head pounding.

Around her there was chatter and soon the sound of ice cubes clinking in glasses. The man in the seat next to her was drinking a Scotch, his knees covered with clipped papers: notes on something. She turned towards the window and closed her eyes again, suddenly feeling desperately tired, both mentally and physically. Once she opened them to see sunlight—her hair was filled with it. It was so bright up there above the clouds and so unreal; a new experience which barely seemed important.

Lunch came round. She toyed with hers, then

realised that she hadn't eaten breakfast and settled for a croissant and butter. Then she must have slipped into an exhausted sleep, waking to discover that the plane was flying steadily over ice floes far below; a broken sea of white, dazzling in the sun, with ribbons of blue sea threading through it. Over Labrador and Greenland and the Hudson, endlessly on, until later they crossed the Canadian coast. Below them were lakes, tiny, shining like glass among the forests and small townships and communities, and here and there snow on the ground. Lots of it.

At last—Canada, and now the fear in her heart tightened into a knot once more. She had no way of knowing if her father was still alive, and she felt sick at the thought, and very alone.

After another two hours she was made aware of the jagged, snow-covered mountains of the Rockies by the captain's voice over the intercom as he told them they were now flying over the tops of them. She found their wild beauty frightening and Canada, for her, unwelcoming. And later, when his voice again commanded their attention, they were told that the plane would land at Vancouver Airport in thirty minutes' time.

Quite suddenly her neighbouring passenger, who hadn't spoken all the way across the Atlantic, put his papers and books away and asked if it was her first visit to Canada.

'Visiting or on holiday?' he went on when she had nodded.

'Visiting—I suppose.'

'Are you being met at the airport?'

'No.' She turned away, refusing to think about it.

He looked at her keenly. 'I was wondering, if you don't know the city perhaps we can drop you somewhere. My wife will be meeting me at the terminal.'

Sarah hesitated. 'I have to take a yellow cab to get into the city?'

He nodded. 'Yes. And it is quite a long way. Stay with me.'

A desperate need not to be alone made her accept gratefully. It was only a short walk into the terminal building and she was even more grateful to the unassuming stranger at her side for showing her the arrival procedure. But at last they emerged—she bewildered—into the reception hall, where the noise seemed deafening, to be greeted within seconds by a casually dressed woman, obviously Sarah's escort's wife, who didn't bat an eyelid when he said easily, 'This is Miss Hillier, darling. We're giving her a lift into the city. It's her first visit to Canada.'

'Hello, there.' Blue, wide-apart eyes gave Sarah a quick assessment and saw no immediate danger as she said, 'Come along, then. The car is parked quite close. Where do you want to be dropped off?'

'I'm not sure. You see, I have to go straight to the hospital.'

'Oh—which one?' They both looked at her.

She opened her bag and took out the information she had been given last night. 'If it's out of your way, I can get a cab.'

'We're taking you right there,' the man insisted firmly. His keen eyes had already diagnosed that she was in some kind of shock on the plane, which was why he had spoken to her. If he hadn't been so immersed in the notes and data of his seminar in London, he might have noticed it before. He had simply thought she was dozing and thanked his lucky stars that he hadn't an infant crawling over him all the way across as he had on the way out.

He elected to drive and as the car swept out on to the highway he looked over his shoulder.

'Perhaps I can help, Miss Hillier. I'm on the medical faculty at this hospital. Dr Sutcliffe. Flying six thousand miles over here must mean an emergency of some kind, I think.'

'Oh—Dr Sutcliffe. . .' Here was the world she knew. 'Do you know Dr Patterson?'

'Neil Patterson? Yes. He's a colleague.'

'He phoned to tell me that my father is in intensive care here and—said I should come right away.'

'Ah.' He turned to his wife. 'Andrea, do you mind driving while I sit in the back with Miss Hillier?'

'Of course not. . .'

Sarah's voice was a broken, unbelieving whisper as she explained; then Andrea Sutcliffe commented, 'I am so sorry. What a fraught time you must have had. And to have come all this way. Have you no one else?'

She shook her head. 'Distant cousins in Australia, I think, but my grandparents are no longer alive. So— there's only me. I'm so afraid I won't be in time. . .'

'You do realise that your father may be comatose? That is to say——'

'I know what it means, Dr Sutcliffe.'

'Look—I want to help. My wife will second this, won't you, Andrea? We shall give you our phone number and address so that you won't feel you have nowhere to go after the hospital. You can trust us to give you any help you may need. Vancouver is no place to be alone. Even hotels can be lonely places at times.'

'I agree,' his wife said huskily. 'Charles will do all he can, I know. I'm so very sorry.'

Sarah couldn't speak. She was aware of their driving across a long bridge, of buildings coming into view, of tall skyscrapers on the skyline and towering blue and grey mountains, snow-capped and gleaming in the afternoon sun.

She no longer tried to keep up with the time change, vaguely thinking that it would be nightfall in England now. Ghost time—where did those hours go?

Her eyes filled with tears as she remembered why she was here. Dr Sutcliffe gripped her hand. 'It's healthier to cry,' he said quietly, seeing her effort to control them. 'Get it over—it's nature's way. We don't mind.'

'I know,' she sobbed. How often she had held the hand of a patient's relative and said the same words.

She was also having to get used to being driven on the opposite side of the road. It was very noisy, with blaring horns and traffic moving in all directions, but when they were approaching the hospital at last she recognised the familiar signs and they were turning on to the forecourt then, and Dr Sutcliffe was helping her out.

A numb coldness enveloped her. She heard him say to his wife, 'Wait for me, Andrea. I'll just take this young lady up to IC, then I'll be back.'

'See that she has our number, Charles.'

'OK.'

'Thank you for everything,' Sarah said.

'Glad we could help, honey. See you later.'

'Hospitals aren't the most welcoming places, but necessary, just the same.' He led the way in. 'We're rather proud of this one.'

'I'm used to this atmosphere, Dr Sutcliffe. I am a nurse back at home.'

'That will certainly stand you in good stead,' he told her, leading the way into a lift which took them immediately to the fourth floor. They emerged into a corridor with a white shining floor, their feet making no sound as they went through double doors and into the intensive care unit.

Dr Sutcliffe asked her to wait in one of the armchairs around the lounge area while he went into a room at the end. Sarah saw a white-coated man coming back with him. His shoulders were well back, and his dark head held high.

Her hand was grasped by cool, strong fingers. 'Hello,' he said quietly. 'I'm Neil Patterson.'

She saw the concern in his dark eyes as she searched

his face for news which she was inwardly dreading to
be told. The room misted slightly and she swayed.

'Hold on, Miss Hillier.' His voice came from a
distance as she was propelled along to his room and
gently lowered into a chair. A nurse was there too. Dr
Sutcliffe had gone.

She heard him ask the nurse to rustle up some
coffee. 'Strong.' Then, as the room cleared, saw that
he was leaning against his desk, watching her.

'I'm sorry. . .' Her voice still seemed too faint, but
as composure returned she knew that she could cope
now.

'No apologies needed,' he said quietly. 'I just wish I
had better news for you. I didn't imagine you would
get here so quickly. Dr Sutcliffe tells me that you are a
professional nurse, which greatly relieves the situation
for me, though not for you. Because naturally you will
want to know the exact nature of your father's injuries.'

'Yes. But first—can I see him?' she pleaded.

'I have to warn you that he is comatose. There are
severe head injuries and—I'm afraid—some inevitable
brain damage.'

'Oh—no—no. . .' He heard the despair in her voice
as this new blow struck home. She knew only too well
the prognosis.

He came nearer and put his hand on her shoulder. 'I
wish I could wrap this up a little, Nurse Hillier, but
you know there is no way I can do that, don't you?'
His voice was quiet and controlled. 'I wasn't sure
yesterday when he came in but now we know the brain
damage to be severe.'

'My father is so vital—a clever man in his field. . .'
she whispered. 'He couldn't bear it if. . . Oh—I don't
think I can take this. . .' She covered her face with her
hands.

His hand was comforting. 'Just live through one hour
at a time,' he said softly. 'Come and see him, then you
must get some rest. I have an appointment now but

don't leave without seeing me. Just ask a nurse to contact me.'

She watched his white-coated figure go away. She could remember only his hands after a while, and that he was taller than herself, and that his eyes were dark and searching.

Her concentration now was on her father's white face, spliced with cuts; his hands too. She shuddered. There was so much she didn't yet know. If only he would just open his eyes and see her, hear her. But the familiar oxygen machine and monitoring instruments and the needle jagging across the chart registering the heartbeats told her everything, and she knew as well as Dr Patterson what his chances were. But it was so hard to believe.

A nurse brought more coffee, and an hour later Dr Patterson himself. He put his hand under Sarah's arm and she went with him unprotestingly.

'Dr Sutcliffe has been on the phone,' he told her gently. 'They would like you to stay with them for a day or two, until you get your bearings. I think that's a sensible thing to do right now too.' He glanced at his watch. 'I'm free for a couple of hours so I'll run you over to their home. It's only ten minutes from here. They live up in the hills a little.'

He had gone on talking to give her time to adjust, she knew that. To agree to leave her father's bedside.

'You need some sleep.' His voice was firm now. 'You can come back in the morning. I'll call you if necessary.'

She didn't say anything to that. She couldn't as he held her coat for her and gave her the shoulder-bag.

'My luggage. . .?'

'They took it on with them, apparently. It will be there waiting for you.'

'Everyone is so kind—I just don't know what to say.'

'Then don't try.'

They came out through a different side-entrance and

he led the way to his car; then she was getting into a low, sports-type Cougar, the long bonnet seeming to rise up with its bouncy suspension, so that even as he drove out through the gates she felt a little car-sick, realising that she had eaten practically nothing except that on the plane. The car turned in the opposite direction from the way she had come in, rising up between glorious colours on the trees dripping with yellow and pink blossom. Every garden had flowers and hedges and hanging baskets and more trees; the maples and budding aspens—which he pointed out to her.

Anything to distract her from the abyss of despair, even a little, into which she kept sliding so helplessly from seeing the father she adored just lying there and unable to speak to her.

The Sutcliffes' house on the city outskirts was perched on the side of a hill which led eventually to the mountains behind. The air was so pure it took her breath away when she got out of the car in the driveway. She exclaimed at the view way below. The river threading on down towards the sea; the pulsing city away to the left. And the mountains all around, towering above everything.

Mrs Sutcliffe came to meet her. 'I'm so glad you decided to come,' she said. 'Come along into the house. Charles is in the lounge, Neil; go and have a drink with him while we go upstairs and we'll join you later. This way—can I call you Sarah?'

'Of course. Please do.'

She wondered vaguely how Andrea Sutcliffe knew her name. How fortunate she had been that Dr Sutcliffe had sat next to her and spoken to her on the plane. It had made everything that much simpler—the trauma of finding her own way to the hospital, for one thing.

Andrea opened a door on the landing. 'Here is your room. The bathroom is next door. I think you'll find everything you need, Sarah. Come down when you're ready, won't you?'

Again she murmured her thanks.

'You're very welcome.'

The door closed and she was alone for the first time since setting foot on Canadian soil. But now that she could shed those tight, welled-up tears, she stared, dry-eyed, at her two cases before unstrapping one of them and searching for her toilet-bag. Just as mechanically she went to find the bathroom for the luxury of washing her face. Then she brushed her hair until the stiff muscles of her neck began to relax, although her head was still pounding. But she changed into a fresh cream silk blouse and beige trousers before going downstairs to where the voices of the others came from a room at the back overlooking the garden. She felt that she was waiting for something with dread. She couldn't think very logically. All so unlike her normal self.

Both men got up for her. She looked from one intelligent face to the other, neither of which she had known this time yesterday.

'What would you like to drink?' Dr Sutcliffe asked quietly. 'I suggest a Scotch and soda. . .'

Sarah took it. 'Thank you. Oh, dear—that's all I seem to be saying, but I am so grateful for everything.'

'I think we should dispense with the thanks,' he insisted, indicating a seat on the chesterfield. 'Dr Patterson and I both feel you should get some rest before going back to the hospital.'

She looked down into her glass. 'I'd like to be there, just in case he. . .' Her eyes closed against the sudden rush of tears. Oh—this was hopeless.

Neil Patterson said briskly, 'Come in for an hour after supper; tomorrow you can stay in one of the guest-rooms we have until we see how things are going. It's usual procedure as you probably know.'

'I'd like to do that,' she said, looking straight at him for the first time and noticing the way his dark hair fell naturally over his forehead and the eyes which were trained to see more than was on the surface. A good doctor's face, the kind she was used to.

He stood up suddenly. 'Thanks for the drink,' he said abruptly. 'See you tomorrow, Charles. I'm impatient to hear about the seminar and what London looks like these days. Haven't been over there for three years. It's my turn next.'

'Well, one thing I knew when I went over to Regent Street to do some shopping for Andrea, there are more foreigners in that street than British, that's for sure. We tend to forget that.'

When Sarah had returned from the hospital later that night after finding her father's condition unchanged, her host insisted on her going straight to bed, and the moment she slipped under the duvet she unexpectedly slept from sheer exhaustion.

When she awoke in the strange room next morning it all came back too clearly and she had to get up straight away. Pushing her feet into mules and tying her dressing-gown around her even smaller waist today, she went in search of any news of her father. Could she call the hospital yet? Was it too early?

But already there were voices coming from the kitchen. Dr Sutcliffe was squeezing oranges and his wife was scrambling eggs. Both wore dressing-gowns. His was blue and very short which, with his slightly tousled hair, gave him a new image. But their welcome dispelled any embarrassment she might feel at her intrusion.

'Come in, Sarah. Orange juice? We didn't know if you were awake yet. Sit down. Andrea is doing scrambled eggs. Must have something to face the day with. How did you sleep?'

'I was so tired. I don't remember anything. Dr Sutcliffe—is there any news?'

'I phoned myself, just now. Nothing has changed. You're going in this morning?'

'Yes. I'm staying there.'

His wife brought her breakfast. 'You will come back for anything you need, won't you? Leave your cases in your room.'

'I don't know how to repay you.'

'No way. . .' Dr Sutcliffe picked up his second cup of coffee. 'I'll take this up with me. I'm operating at eight-thirty this morning. Andrea will run you in to the hospital when she goes shopping. Try not to worry more than you must. It—isn't going to change anything, you know.'

'He's so kind,' Sarah commented as she finished her coffee.

'He's the best,' his wife answered. 'And he's right. It won't change anything, only undermine your strength. Your father doesn't know what is happening right now. Only you know, and for you it's a waiting time. You're strong, honey. You'll live through it. I know. It happened to me in almost the same way. My mother had a heart attack and there was nothing anyone could do. So I know how you're feeling. Can you be ready at nine?'

It was different this morning, finding her own way to the fourth floor. The nurses here all wore white overalls and caps and white shoes, and on the way up in the lift Sarah learned that Dr Sutcliffe was a consultant here at the hospital. But otherwise it was like any hospital.

A nurse took her along to her father's room. She asked if there was any change and was told that there was not.

'I see. Thanks.' She hadn't thought there would be.

She talked to him, yet knew he could not hear. He looked even thinner today and so quiet, so still. She felt helpless. Surely there was something she could do? She just could not sit there hour after hour and do nothing. If she could help nurse him—even in an unofficial capacity. . . Would they let her?

Dr Patterson came in to look at him and after

glancing at his notes looked up when Sarah got up to leave. 'Don't go. You can help me with him if you like.'

Quickly and without fuss she did what he asked. He gave her a discerning look, his brow creased slightly. 'Come along to my room. I've a suggestion to put to you,' he said, and waited for her to join him.

On the way he ordered coffee for them both. 'In my room, please, Nurse.'

She sat in the chair he indicated, facing him, and he shuffled some papers on his desk while the coffee was brought in and the door closed. Then he looked at her.

'You're feeling shattered today, I expect.'

She nodded silently.

'You want to stay near your father, don't you?'

'Oh, yes. I have to.'

'You know as well as I do that this could go on for weeks—or——'

'I know.' Her eyes never left his face. 'I—can't leave him. . .'

'I understand that. What you don't know is that there was another person injured in that same accident. He was driving the other car involved.'

'Was—he badly hurt?'

'Bad enough. He is just along the corridor from your father actually. His name is Mike Rayner and he's a rancher in his thirties. And he has numerous fractures among other quite painful injuries. And he does not take his immobilisation lightly. Which is understandable, as the accident doesn't seem to have been his fault. He's ranting on a bit—and not co-operating.'

'Dad was to blame? Oh—don't you see? That makes it so much worse. . .'

'It seems that he was on the wrong side of the highway. It was inevitable.'

'I see that. I—feel I ought to go and explain to him that Dad wasn't used to your roads. Do you think he would mind? It's the least I can do. To tell him how very sorry I am—and for my father too.'

'If you're feeling brave enough, you can come along with me right now. But I warn you, he's a very angry man and already two nurses have asked to be transferred. Sure you feel up to it?'

She nodded dumbly and saw Dr Patterson smile for the first time as he picked up the rancher's case notes. And that smile transformed his face.

'He also seems to be having girl trouble,' he said. 'Monique rang to say she doesn't like hospitals and does not intend to visit.'

'Oh—that would obviously upset him.'

Mike Rayner's was the last door along the corridor. Sarah soon understood why. Even as they reached it they heard a male voice protesting and the nurse insisting. 'But you must, Mr Rayner. Doctor says so.'

'And I say I won't. Go away—and don't come back.'

The door opened and out she came. Sarah had a full view of the man in the bed, both legs in plaster and strung up in traction, one arm in a sling also in traction, and a cut with several sutures across his forehead.

He glared at them both, frowning.

'Oh, dear. . .' she said softly; then followed behind Dr Patterson into the room, closed the door and waited.

CHAPTER TWO

SARAH was all too familiar with the stark ugliness of burns and the injuries which patients sustained from car accidents. Such casualties had made up a large part of the weekend intake at St David's, especially young motorcyclists.

But this man was different because she already felt personally involved. Now, as she stood beside Dr Patterson, his intensely blue eyes glared back at her from a swollen, discoloured face. Tousled fair hair falling over his forehead reminded her of a vulnerable schoolboy, resentful and sullen as he muttered, 'Oh, no. Who the hell is this now? I don't want any visitors.'

'This,' Neil Patterson said firmly, with the hint of a smile, 'is Miss Sarah Hillier; you don't have to stand on ceremony, I can assure you—so just relax.'

'Is that some kind of joke, Doc?'

'Of course not. I'm glad you're able to talk, Mike. That's something—painful though it must be.'

'God—what a remark. With how many stitches in my face?'

Sarah saw him grimace and knew that the facial abrasions alone must be smarting, searing, each time he moved his mouth as she assessed him professionally from under her dark lashes. He moved his head slightly, resenting her, and it showed.

'Mike,' Neil Patterson said quietly, 'Miss Hillier flew in yesterday from the UK. She wanted to tell you something, if you're up to it.'

'I'm not.'

'OK. Maybe later.' His patient looked up at him, Sarah having already retreated to the door. 'Look— keep those nurses away. I can't stand them flapping

around. I've got this hand. . .' He held up his left one.
'I'll look after my own needs and use my own razor
when they get here with my bag. They *have* been told
at the ranch?' He winced as he put his good hand to
his face, feeling the bristled chin.

'Your stockman I believe is driving down. Joe
somebody?'

'Elliston.'

'Well, before he gets here I'd like you to get some
sleep. I'll give you your jab myself. OK?'

Mike nodded, closing his eyes in mute acceptance,
and Sarah opened the door and went out into the
corridor. Waiting for Dr Patterson, she heard his
patient ask huskily, obviously thinking she was out of
earshot, 'Why was she here?' and Dr Patterson's reply,

'Two reasons actually, Mike. One, I thought as you
were from the UK originally you might find some
common ground, and also because she asked to see
you. Her father was seriously injured in the crash
and—we had to get her over here, fast.'

'It's that serious? He's in this hospital?'

'He's in intensive care. At the end of the corridor.
His daughter is staying in too.'

'Oh. . .' He muttered an expletive. 'He came right
at me, you know. There was no way I could avoid it.'
He shuddered.

'Obviously not your fault, Mike. Now—try to get
some rest, there's a good guy. That's your jab over.
Relax.'

He came out and closed the door. For Sarah, able to
hear every word, it was almost too much, but her eyes
met those of Dr Patterson bravely as she walked beside
him back to her father's room.

'Sorry about that,' he commented. 'He's resentful,
and feeling frustrated right now.'

'Combined with the pain.'

'That too.'

He watched her go back into her father's room, her head bent. Then he continued with his rounds.

Sarah felt grateful that he had given her so much of his time already. And, indefinably, some inner strength, because he seemed to be sharing this tragedy with her. Yet to him her father was just another patient. She didn't feel quite so alone because of Neil Patterson.

But, of course, she was. Because her father didn't even know that she was here beside his bed. Her throat tightened with misery. If he would only open his eyes, just once. If he would smile at her, chuckle the way he used to when he came in at the end of the day. He had been the backbone of her life since she was a small girl. Now nothing could break through the barrier. His injuries were too severe. She clung to his hand, just the same, while her thoughts tried to surface and the future blurred. 'I wish we weren't both so far from home,' she told him, even though he couldn't hear. But who knew for sure about that either? Hearing was the last to go.

It was one of the nurses who dragged her away to the canteen for lunch. 'You have to come. It's doctor's orders. . .' she insisted, and Sarah had to admit that the hum of conversation and chatter of crockery was so reminiscent of St David's that she slipped into it quite naturally, though she wasn't hungry—and ate little.

'So—you're a nurse too. Dr Patterson just told me. I'm Debby Howe.'

'Sarah. It's nice to know you, Debby. Thanks for being so kind,' she ended gratefully.

'You're having a really bad time, aren't you? The worst, I'd say. We'd all like to help—so just ask for anything. Where are you staying? A hotel?'

'No. With Dr Sutcliffe and his wife.'

'Gee—how did that come about?'

'I came over on the same plane with him. I had no idea who he was until he spoke to me at the airport and discovered I was coming here to the hospital. His wife was so nice to me. I was in some kind of shock, I suppose; couldn't get to grips with—oh, I still can't.'

'You need a sedative, honey.'

'No. I don't want anything. I'm not desperate. I didn't get much sleep last night, which was only to be expected. The Sutcliffes have been marvellous. So has Dr Patterson. Now—I'd better get back, Debby,' she finished apologetically. 'I can't eat any more—and my father just might. . .'

The nurse with her didn't comment as they left. They both knew it was almost impossible for David Hillier to regain full consciousness again. But stranger things had happened in surgery. So long as there was a thread of life to hang on to.

'You haven't met our patient in room six yet, have you?' Debby was saying as they turned the corridor. 'Well, you wouldn't; he only came in the day before yesterday and he's already gone through two nurses and a special whom Dr Patterson called in today. I guess he's quite a nice guy usually, but he sure is irascible right now.'

'Understandably, I should think,' Sarah said grimly, refusing to let her thoughts dwell on him, shutting out his challenging, angry blue eyes. He didn't want to know her, and why should he?

There was a phone message from Dr Sutcliffe saying that he would pick her up at six. She was to go home for a meal with his wife and himself and collect anything she might need before returning to the hospital. She guessed that they also wanted to see how she was holding up after today.

At five, Dr Patterson came to look at her father, together with two interns. She made for the door as he began to discuss her father's case with them, quietly closing it behind her before going to the windows and gazing across at mountains wreathed in mist now, unfriendly, unfamiliar and totally different from what she had imagined, as was the city—what she had seen of it so far. So huge, such tall skyscraper buildings, with glimpses of sandy beaches, a short way from the busy, hustling, unceasing streams of traffic in the centre of the city. And lots of colour everywhere. Neon signs dazzling all the time, vying with the more quiet greens of the trees around the foothills of the mountains. It was difficult to absorb the fact that she was here in Canada at all; the other side of the world and so far from England and home.

Her throat ached with strangled realisation. Home— how could it ever be that for her again? How could she go back there without him?

As she turned away from the misty mountains across the water, she saw the interns disappearing down the corridor towards Mike Rayner's room, to what kind of reception she could only guess while she went back to sit with her father again, sliding her fingers into his irresponsive hand, for her own comfort mainly.

She wished she could do something to help Mike Rayner. And resisted a strong compulsion to go along to his room again and try to explain. But there was no way she could do that without permission. The feeling remained. Why did she feel so responsible towards him? As if she too were partly to blame for his injuries, for his being there. Surely he must know how she felt at seeing him lying there immobile and in pain, knowing that her father was the cause?

It was an accident, she kept telling herself. But it didn't change anything.

It was almost six. She must go. Doctor Sutcliffe would be waiting. There was nothing she could do here. She would know. Wearily, she went to the door as a nurse came in to check everything after giving her a sympathetic smile.

As she reached Dr Patterson's room, he saw her and came out. He immediately gave her the latest report on her father, sparing nothing. Sarah knew it all herself anyway. It was acceptance which was hard.

She thanked him quietly. His eyes never left her face, so pale, her eyes larger than ever, framed in the soft brown hair curling into her neck.

'Dr Sutcliffe is coming for me but I will be back,' she said. Just then he came striding across the floor towards them.

'It's raining outside. Come along, Sarah, it will do you good to get some fresh air. You'll be coming back, I guess.'

'Yes, I have to.'

'Sure.'

'OK. . .' Neil Patterson broke in '. . .but you're to go to bed properly. It's been quite a day for you and I insist.' His voice was gentle in spite of its firmness and she flashed him a grateful look, to see real concern in the dark eyes.

'You've been so kind. Everyone has. . .'

'Try to get some rest tonight,' he said gently. As she left he watched her thoughtfully until they were both in the lift; and his expression was quite unreadable.

Sarah too was deep in thought as she walked with the surgeon over to his car. In some strange context she felt that she and Neil Patterson had never been strangers. It was as if he had come to her by design. She was too tired to question it further. Fortunately, Dr Sutcliffe was not given to small talk and she didn't expect it, knowing he couldn't switch off from a heavy day in theatre any more than she could drag herself from a deep well of apprehension and sadness.

The surgeon was aware of this. It wasn't over for Sarah yet and he felt deeply sorry for her. She might have been his daughter. That really brought it home to him, and his voice was very gentle as he helped her out when they reached the house among the trees, which were dripping now in the early evening rain, making the flowers in the borders even brighter by contrast, their scent clinging. They went inside where a meal was waiting for them.

At eight, Andrea drove her back to the hospital. In her Sarah found a sympathetic friend and she promised to keep in touch through the next few days, even if she didn't get away from the hospital.

The rest of the evening was fairly quiet. Interns and nurses alike treated her as one of themselves now and she was only too glad to help with her father's care: changing sheets, even helping to wash him. She felt integrated as she sat watching the EKG tracing his heartbeats. In an English hospital it would be known as an ECG; electrocardiograph. In fact, she was learning that quite a few things over here were given different names. But a hospital was a hospital, her normal habitat. Sometimes her thoughts moved along the corridor to where, it was now accepted, was the most difficult patient they had handled for a long time.

When a male nurse came out of his room she tentatively asked how he was making out.

'Gee—he's one angry guy. Did you hear him grinding away at me just now?'

She said, 'No. I expect he hates all this confinement.'

'Sure. But will he give in and have some sedation? No, sir! He's some fighter. Can't help liking the guy though.'

'Which reminds me. . .' Sister-in-charge had come across to them and heard the last part of their conversation '. . . Dr Patterson left instructions that you are to take these two tablets at ten. It's that now, so off to bed with you. That's an order, Nurse Hillier. The second on the right is your room.'

It was the prefix which did it, together with the disorientation of both her mind and body. She gave in gratefully, sliding between cool sheets; somewhere in the hospital precincts an ambulance siren blared, but she was already drifting into sleep by then. She knew they would call her if any change occurred in her father's condition.

It was seven-thirty in the morning when she awoke drowsily, surprised to find that it was the night sister herself who had brought her some coffee, shaking her head in answer to her first question. She looked grave. 'Not anything definite,' she said slowly; then, more briskly, 'If you'd like a bath or shower—right next door to you. I should get it over before things start to hot up. And then go for some breakfast. We don't want another patient on our hands. You do need to keep up your strength, you know.'

'Everyone is so kind, Sister. I don't want to be any trouble.'

'This is a special floor—and as a qualified nurse you should know that it's somewhat different from any-where else in the hospital,' she remarked, closing the door after her.

Sarah nodded, her eyes clouding over. She did know—only too well—why she was here as an in-visitor, and St David's somehow seemed part of a distant past. Long ago, she had driven her father's car out through the huge iron gates on a sun-dappled evening, with all the promise of spring and summer ahead. A time to make plans, take stock; which she had, with no thought of tragedy. How complacent can you get? she thought miserably as she tied her house-coat around her waist and took a towel and her wash-bag, going immediately into the quiet, orderly, busy hospital routine of the intensive care unit.

Later that day her father's condition worsened and Sarah didn't leave his bedside.

Dr Patterson was in theatre all morning and part of the afternoon. It was almost five when she heard his footsteps along the corridor. He came to stand beside her, wordlessly.

Just at that moment her father stopped breathing and quietly slipped away. Neil reached down and took her cramped fingers from his hand and held them in his own.

'It's over for him,' he said gently, and as Sister came into the room and their eyes met, he put his hand under Sarah's elbow and led her towards his room. He was her strength then.

She heard him asking for hot strong tea to be sent in to them. Sister came and held her shoulder against her white dress until she stopped trembling.

'It's best this way,' she said consolingly.

'I know.' And of course, she did know, and that it had been inevitable right from the time of the accident.

'And you were here with him,' Sister reminded her.

'Yes.'

Neil Patterson poured the tea himself, looking across at Sister. 'You can go, if you have something you want to do,' he said tactfully. 'No need to stay. I'll be here for a while yet.'

'Good. But get to me if I can help,' she said, looking at Sarah.

'Thank you, Sister. For everything. I'll be all right now.'

Neil Patterson perched on the edge of his table while her trembling fingers took the hot tea. Then he picked up his own and watched her carefully. 'I don't know your plans, Sarah, but there are some decisions you have to make almost right away. It's best to get the formalities over at once, but there have to be some things connected with the accident which can't be concluded yet.'

'I understand,' she said quietly.

'If you are planning to return to the UK. . . Are you?'

'I don't know. . .' She passed her hand wearily over her forehead.

'If so, you must get a flight booked. I thought you might be flying back to England. Your father. . . It has to be thought about, Sarah. I am so sorry you have to face up to all this alone. Remember that I'm here and that I want to help. I do mean that.'

She got up then. 'I'm taking up your time—I know that.'

He pushed her gently back into her chair. 'Not at all. And I intend taking you back to the Sutcliffes' house when you feel able to go.'

'I am grateful for that. Thank you.' Her swimming eyes met his. He saw the effort she was making into pulling herself together. Her long lashes swept her cheeks, tears still clinging to them, and she never knew the effect she was having on the surgeon at that moment.

'Get your coat,' he said quietly, resisting the desire to put his arms around her and cradle her against his white coat, giving her the physical comfort she needed so badly just then. 'I'll wait for you here. Then we'll go straight back.'

He opened the door for her, touching her shoulder as she passed. Then he went straight to his desk and called Andrea Sutcliffe on the phone. Their conversation, though quite short, relieved him of some of the responsibility he felt towards Sarah.

He didn't attempt to make conversation on the short journey, concentrating on the highway, misty with rain sweeping in from the mountains, apart from asking her once if she was OK.

She nodded, her, 'Yes—thank you,' just a whisper. It was still so hard to accept, and other thoughts were beginning to flash across her mind now. Suddenly there seemed so much to do. So many decisions which must be made, and they were mainly all down to her.

That kind of trauma had been part of her job back at St David's. Something she had been trained to do, only this was different. Her own trauma.

Andrea was waiting for her, the door open, and Neil, coming round to open the car door for her, saw a more resigned look on her face as he took hold of her hand to help her out, because her legs seemed like lead and suddenly tension and anxiety had caught up with her. She went slowly into the house and Andrea's arms were around her in a wordless hug.

She heard the car rev up and belatedly realised that she had forgotten to thank him.

That night the Sutcliffes were both there to give her help in advising her about the formalities which had to be gone through. Sarah was more than grateful to them for this. Neither did they try to pressure her into eating or even talking if she didn't want to.

'I don't know what I've done to deserve two people like you,' she told them, gathering new strength from their back-up. 'I've known you for such a short time and yet. . .'

'We are both glad to help. Think nothing of it,' Charles Sutcliffe said firmly. 'Get some sleep and leave any other decisions until the morning.'

'I have to make some phone calls to England, Dr Sutcliffe. It will be five in the morning over there so that too must wait, I think, until tomorrow.'

'Good girl.'

'Do you mind if I go to bed now?' She dreaded being alone but needed to be.

'Surely not. Will you sleep?'

'I'll try. Goodnight.'

When she reached the top of the thickly carpeted staircase she pushed open her door, closing it quietly behind her. Only then did she cry: great sobbing tears for her father and for herself and for all the years when he wouldn't be there. Why—why did it have to happen this way? There was no answer to that. There never was.

Andrea drove her into the hospital next morning to collect some necessary papers and her father's belongings, after which there would be the final arrangements to be made. Sarah had not yet called her father's solicitors in England.

Leaving Andrea in the cafeteria to have coffee, she made her way to the top floor. As yet she had told no one about her thoughts, the unreality of them, during the long sleepless night. And the decisions she had reached. But, as always, she had faced up to reality and she knew that she wanted her father to stay here. At rest. There was no way she could face the trauma of taking his body back to England and the subsequent drawn-out arrangements which would have to be made there.

Neither did she herself want to go back there. Not yet. It had come to her, as she'd lain staring out at the black starry sky in the early hours, that he would be quietly resting in that green tree-filled cemetery on the hill with the tiny church near by. If it was at all possible, that was what she wanted for him.

The lift doors closed silently behind her and she stepped out into the corridor, into the medical atmosphere she knew, her own background: the smell, the trolleys and linen-packed shelves glimpsed through open doorways, oxygen tanks, nurses silently coming and going; closed doors bearing patients' names, telephones, doctors' rooms and, right at the end, the ICU.

She didn't know if it would be possible to see Neil Patterson today. She couldn't disturb him anyway and he just could be in theatre. There were voices from room six as she reached it—Mike Rayner's room—and, as she passed by, the door opened rather suddenly and the surgeon came out, his expression more frustrated than angry, but certainly a good mixture of both. He was shaking his head in disbelief, until he saw her and quickly gained control again. 'Hello, Sarah. Were you coming to see me?'

'I—hoped you might spare a few minutes,' she began, 'but I have to collect my father's things and. . .'

'Come into my office. I have an appointment at ten. Does that give us time to talk?'

'Yes. I won't keep you long.'

'How are you? Did you sleep?'

She shook her head. 'There is something I want to ask you about. I know I'm taking advantage of your——'

'No,' he said, closing his office door. 'What is it? I did offer to help in any way.'

She told him then about her decision. He saw the effort she was making to stay calm and not let her grief intrude. He watched her thoughtfully.

'You see—I don't want to go back yet either. I—don't feel ready for that somehow.'

'I understand that, Sarah. Will you take leave of absence indefinitely?'

'I don't know. Yes—I suppose that would be best. I haven't called them yet.'

'Sarah—you know as well as I that you have to be in an emotional state of mind. Don't make any final decisions yet, except those which have to be made. Because of the accident there will be, I'm afraid, investigations and statements from Mike Rayner, among other things. It all takes time. Just get through this week—it will be your worst yet.'

'My father doesn't need me any more,' she said bravely. 'I know that work is the best therapy and—oh, is there any way I can help Mike Rayner? If it's at all possible, will you consider me if and when you need another nurse? I've thought about this all night and it's something I have to do.'

'I don't believe this. . . Are you quite sure that you've given it sufficient thought?'

'Yes.' She had already seen the look of relief crossing his face.

'Do you realise that he's just gone through yet another agency nurse? Admin can't get anyone to stay for more than a day. Do you feel up to coping with

him? It's a challenge, believe me, but you just might
be able to get through to him that he needs a resident
nurse. For the present time, anyway. I can have a word
with Administration if you would like to contact them
later. You just might be what we need right now. You
do have something, perhaps. Would you like to have
more time to think, Sarah?'

'I already have thought. This is something I have to
do. Please understand. I have to. . .'

'I think I do. We'll be in touch, you know that, don't
you?'

Her eyes met his for a moment. 'Yes,' she said
almost in a whisper, and left, not looking back. If she
had she would have seen that he followed her out into
the corridor and watched her retreating figure disbelievingly, before glancing at his watch and going back
into his office and pressing his bell for his duty nurse.

Sarah collected the holdall containing her father's
things and went down in the lift to find Andrea. 'I'm so
sorry. . .' she began, but Andrea hadn't minded at all.
She had been in conversation with someone she hadn't
seen for quite a time.

'I've enjoyed talking over old times,' she said happily. 'Janet was a sister here when she and I worked
together. That's a long time ago. Now she comes in
sometimes and does voluntary work on the geriatric
floor. Besides, you've only been fifteen minutes. Did
you manage to see Neil Patterson?'

'Yes. I did, and I have something to tell you.'

She stood there, clutching her father's holdall, her
face pale and strained.

'I have to make special arrangements for my father's
funeral, Andrea. Will you—come with me?'

'Of course, honey. Of course.' She slipped her arm
through Sarah's and they went out to the car parked
on the fore-court. 'Now—what do you have to tell me,
Sarah?'

CHAPTER THREE

BACK at the house, Sarah immediately began her calls to England. Mr Attwood had to come first, though she realised, after dialling his number from the back of her diary, that he would very probably not still be in his office. It was almost seven in the evening over there in the UK.

But it was his familiar voice answering, sounding almost as if he were in the next room. And what she had to tell him became even more difficult because her throat ached with suppressed tears. He had always been a familiar figure to the family and was, of course, very shocked to hear about her father. Even more so when she said that she would not be bringing him home for his funeral.

'I will have to leave announcements and everything else in your hands,' she told him. He agreed to notify the bank and take over all legalities and, with the Sutcliffes' telephone number in front of him, it was comforting for Sarah to know that he was only at the other end of a cable any time she needed to talk to him. 'Thank you, Mr Attwood,' she said bravely. 'I do assure you that I have strong reasons for wanting to remain here in Vancouver for a time. I am sure you will understand when I can tell you about them.'

'So you won't be returning to St David's, then, Sarah? Do they know that?'

'No. I have to get in touch with them next through my ward sister.'

Telling Sister Maine was another matter. She was already home from the hospital. Her voice too seemed very close.

'Oh, Sarah, how dreadful for you. But I did realise

36

how seriously hurt he must have been for them to have
sent for you. I am so sorry, my dear. So—what are
your immediate plans? When will you be flying back
with——?'

'No, Sister. I—have decided that, after all the formalities and enquiries have been made, my father's
funeral will take place here.'

'I see. Well, that means you will ask for extended
leave, of course. Shall I get it under way for you? Is
there some special reason for—not bringing him back
here? I'm sure there must be.'

'Yes, Sister. There is. But I can't go into it. It's just
that right now I feel I am needed here. It's something
I have to do. And—not extended leave, Sister. I'm
leaving St David's. A—clean break. I don't know how
long I will stay over here. However long it takes. I will
be back some time, of course. And we'll meet then.
I'm—sorry, Sister.'

'Oh, Sarah, so am I. Please, please keep in touch.'

'You know I will. Goodbye, now. I'll write to the
head nursing officer myself.'

Andrea called her from the kitchen. It was evident
that the strain was building up again. She had prepared
a light lunch for them both, and hoped Sarah would
relax a little.

'I've poured you some white wine. It will give you
some appetite, honey. You have to keep your strength
up, you know. It's been quite a morning.'

For herself as well as Sarah, because she had also
been thrown by her decision to have her father buried
here in Vancouver. She was also very impressed by
Sarah's firm commitment and her decision to stay here
and see it through. There had been nothing hysterical
about it. She had simply said, 'It would be what my
father would have wanted me to do,' and if there was
a break in her voice, she had quickly overcome it.

'I understand,' Andrea had told her and, actually,
she did.

When the phone rang and she answered, she came to tell Sarah that Neil Patterson had called. 'He's on the phone now. He wants a word.'

She found his voice vaguely comforting. 'Sarah—I'm just out of theatre for a few minutes but I thought I'd better warn you that you will probably receive a call from Administration this afternoon. What you decide to do is entirely up to you, but I think they may try to persuade you to start work fairly soon.'

'Oh. Well, thanks for warning me. I shall be here if they call me.'

'How are you feeling?' She couldn't not hear the note of concern in his voice, somehow sounding even more intimate over the phone.

'I'm—fine, thanks. Really. It's as you said, one hour at a time, and then the next.'

'Good. Have to go. I'm in theatre today. I'll—be in touch.'

She went back to the kitchen, feeling strangely comforted just from speaking to him. A vision of him in theatre garb in her mind gave her cause once again to feel grateful that he had taken the trouble to contact her, so that when the hospital phoned later she was prepared. She had to see the nursing officer at four, and Administration after that if possible.

'I'll drive you in to the hospital,' Andrea told her. 'Only if you feel up to it.'

She took a deep breath. 'Oh, yes. I want to get on with it.'

'OK, honey.'

At four o'clock she sat quietly in an outer office waiting to finalise starting work in this hospital. It was all beginning to seem unreal, as if she were on the outside looking in. The events of the day could have belonged to someone else and yet, here in this almost familiar environment, one she had been used to all her adult life, she felt somehow secure and it was hard to imagine that thousands of miles divided her now from

St David's. Last week she hadn't even heard of this place.

In the event the interview was fairly short because the senior nursing officer was in possession of all the facts and her own schedule very tight.

'I will need a work permit, won't I?' Sarah asked her.

She nodded. 'And an authorisation, which I will get on to right away. In these special circumstances I am confident it will be straightforward. So—when would you like to start?'

'Tomorrow?'

'So soon? Are you sure you feel up to it? It would be fine if you could.'

'Yes. It—may even help to. . .'

'Therapeutically, I'm sure it will, Nurse. You won't have uniform, of course, so I will get someone to take you along to have yours fitted. Report to Sister-in-charge now, and—good luck.'

Sarah left the office, throwing her head back and taking a deep breath. It was just the kind of thing she used to say to her juniors if they were having personal problems: 'Work is the best therapy. You will soon feel better.' Well, now it applied to herself and right now her throat ached with unshed tears and she didn't feel better.

Instead of taking the lift she walked down the stairs to the floor below. Here she would be working from tomorrow onwards. Charge Sister was in her office writing but got up at once when she saw Sarah.

'So, you're taking over our problem patient, Nurse. There are also three other patients along that corridor. Part of the time you will be nursing them too. Did you know that?'

'No. But I do now, Sister.'

'Oh, Mr Rayner doesn't have exclusive rights to you, but I'm quite sure he'll be taking up far more of your time than they. All Dr Patterson's patients, of course. Those are his wards usually.'

'Yes. I see,' she murmured, wondering why she hadn't realised that they would also be included in her schedule. Not that it mattered, and was only to be expected.

'Nurse Williams will also be working with you,' Sister concluded, 'but not in Mr Rayner's case. He will be under your care and the night staff's. Good nursing, Sarah. I hope you can subdue him somewhat—not too much; just enough to get his medication into him and monitoring and dressings taken care of. Oh—by the way, Dr Sutcliffe is picking you up at the side-door at six o'clock. That gives you time to sort out your uniform first.'

'Thank you, Sister. Goodbye.'

Just before six she sat in the waiting-room where Dr Sutcliffe would find her. Everything had been settled. Tomorrow would find her here as one of the staff. Her thoughts mulled over her immediate problems. The hospital bill, for one thing, which must have soared. And other necessary expenses which depended on finance.

Her father's bank and Mr Attwood would give her any help and advice, she knew. After all, they were only a phone call away. A sudden vision of the offices in the country high street in summer, with wistaria hanging in blue clusters from the front of the old Georgian house, brought an immediate nostalgia. But no tears. Somehow they seemed to have become frozen into a hard knot of apprehension instead. It would get better one day, she thought wistfully. Just now she was feeling very alone.

But Neil Patterson, leaving the lift and heading for the way out, saw her at once. The slightly bent head, her hair tumbling over her forehead and, as he reached her, the disconsolate expression on her face reflected her thoughts. Neil had been thinking about her as he'd stood in the lift. Her face was beginning to haunt him, coming at unexpected moments, though he hadn't admitted it yet, even to himself.

Sarah heard him walking across the shining grey floor, although she had no idea it was he until he stopped beside her and she looked up. There was concern in the dark brown eyes and he looked very tired—the drained look of a surgeon who had been operating for most of the day and as yet hadn't had time to relax. It was a clean-cut face, one she had come to trust, and it seemed now that it was one she had always known. Not just for such a time as it actually was. 'You are getting a ride home, Sarah?'

'Yes. Dr Sutcliffe asked me to wait for him.'

'He isn't going to be too much longer. And you're coming in tomorrow to take over some of my patients, and Mike Rayner in particular?'

'Yes. I don't know how it all happened in so short a time, but perhaps it's for the best. I feel it's right for me to. . .'

'I understand how you feel,' he said, 'and it could be that between us we'll get it through to him that he needs round-the-clock nursing care and then it might cease to become a problem. He has to come around to it. But—don't take more from him than you have to. Just come and talk to me about any problems.'

'Thanks. But I don't anticipate anything I can't handle, Dr Patterson. It's a challenge and I'll see it through.'

He smiled then. 'Good girl. Ah—here's Charles now.'

The lift doors opened to disgorge some members of staff, one or two giving Sarah a curious glance as they passed, and lastly Dr Sutcliffe, briefcase in hand.

'Hello there. Sorry to keep you waiting, Sarah. So you're off too, Neil?'

'Yes. But I'll be back later, just to check on my post-ops.'

She walked with them to their respective cars, Neil Patterson giving her a slight smile as he said goodnight.

When she was safely seatbelted Dr Sutcliffe drove out on to the highway, joining the stream of traffic all going in the same direction until he turned away on to the quieter lane leading up to his home, where Andrea was waiting for them.

Quietly they both discussed with her the arrangements she had made that day. The stress and trauma had to take its toll and after supper she went off to her room, leaving the doctor and his wife alone.

Tomorrow was another day, the start of a new era in her life. Had she thought it through enough? They were probably saying the same thing downstairs as they talked together, she guessed, but in her whole being Sarah felt it was right. Besides, inexplicably, she wanted to remain here in Vancouver for a time. But as yet she hadn't gone into the logic behind it, only as far as Mike's recovery was entailed.

She slept from sheer exhaustion eventually and awoke to the smell of coffee wafting up the stairs.

The bathroom was empty, the Sutcliffes' voices coming from the kitchen, so she washed quickly and was ready for breakfast when Andrea called up to her that it was ready and that Charles would be leaving in fifteen minutes.

So—this was it.

While she looked pale, her eyes larger than normal, Sarah had found new motivation. Both of them saw it as she came downstairs, raincoat over her arm. She left it on the chair in the hall and still had time for a snatched breakfast.

When she got to the hospital she soon began to feel more integrated into the atmosphere and especially when she caught sight of Debby, who already knew that she was starting today, and thought she must be crazy.

'Gee—I'm going to watch this particular lion being

tamed,' she said with a grin. 'How are you? Feel up to it?'

'Yes,' Sarah answered firmly. 'I wouldn't be here if I didn't. I'm—glad to be working again. There—it's different, this uniform, but it feels very comfortable.'

'And looks super. I have to go now. I'll look for you at lunchtime in the canteen. I'm in out-patients clinic today.'

Others of the staff began to acknowledge Sarah as she closed her locker door. It was good to be part of a world she knew, she thought, her spirits lifting for a moment.

The uniform certainly helped. Sarah had the right image now. The cap was soon adjusted, the white overall belted and her watch pinned in place. Her brown hair curled out as tantalisingly as ever as she walked along the corridor and breathed deeply enough to get her over the initial moment when she entered the lion's den.

To say Mike Rayner just glared at her was putting it mildly. His face was terribly swollen and discoloured, the sutures in evidence. He wore nothing on the top part of his body—just a sheet over his torso. His chest and shoulders were strongly muscled, healthy and denoting an outdoor man in every sense of the word. But his eyes, so far—blue and almost fierce in their intensity—did not leave her face.

'Hello. . .' she said quietly, assessing his reaction while she smiled down at him, aware of an inner trepidation which threatened to overrule her professional confidence.

'So—what is all this?' he asked, frowning up at her.

'I'm to take over as your immediate nurse on this ward, Mr Rayner.'

He glared at her. 'You're what? Whose idea was this?'

'Dr Patterson's, actually. You need bed nursing, which only a trained nurse can do. I know you hate all this and I'm terribly sorry that it is necessary, but it won't be forever.'

'No way,' he reiterated firmly, grimacing as he did so.

'I'm afraid you don't have much choice. It will be someone else if it isn't me. We want to get you better. Try to co-operate.' She stood her ground, refusing to be intimidated. 'You don't look very comfortable. Has your bed been straightened this morning?'

'It's OK. Leave it. Just—go away!'

She guessed that he hadn't been very co-operative and the night staff had got through as quickly as possible.

She pulled his sheet firmly into place, then went around to the other side and straightened it.

'So,' he asked outrageously, 'what next? I've already been washed, fed, my back rubbed with something obnoxious and as these. . .' he indicated his plastered legs '. . .are to remain undisturbed, I guess, and I have all the other necessary implements to hand—I don't need you, do I, Nurse?'

'You know you do,' she said quietly as she studied his chart.

'What's that for?'

'Your BP.'

'I don't have a raised blood-pressure. Although I'm not sure—guess I could have now.'

She ignored his banter while she unwound the sphygmomanometer and reached for his good arm. He flexed his muscle teasingly. 'You are obviously feeling better,' she observed, watching the needle, her trained eyes noticing as much as she could while he was in a more co-operative mood.

'OK?'

'Fine. . .' It was just slightly up on the early morning's reading. 'Temperature and pulse now.'

Her cool fingers slid around his wrist. She tried to feel completely detached as she watched the second hand on her watch. Then she deliberately went over to the table to fill in his chart before coming back to take the thermometer out of his mouth.

'Your face must be very uncomfortable. . .'

'Yes,' he admitted, 'I guess so.'

'It's the tissues and skin starting to heal. I could put something on for you, if you like. But it's better not to.'

'No.'

'I have to give you an injection. Dr Patterson insists you need it—for the pain.'

'I don't intend to become an addict. No, thanks.'

'It will only be for the first few days. The quieter you are, the quicker the bones will knit together. But if you go on moving around—which must hurt—you stand the chance of their not doing that. It makes sense, Mr Rayner.'

'Mike. OK?'

'OK. Do you want to read, Mike?'

'What with? One hand?'

'It can be done. You don't have anything for distraction. Why not have your radio on? Look—I'll put the switch nearer.'

She slid her arm under his shoulders and literally held him against her cool overall while she moved his pillows more comfortably, turning the top one so that it was fresh. He relaxed against it and closed his eyes as waves of pain enveloped him once more.

Quietly she fetched the syringe dish and found a spot on the back of his upper thigh where the flesh was firm, yet able to take the needle. Gently she pulled the sheet into place. His eyes were still closed, his arrogance temporarily subdued. And he hadn't protested. It was unbelievable. She breathed a great sigh of relief.

When Sarah left room six that evening after handing over to the night staff, she felt that something had definitely been accomplished. There had been outbursts—she had expected those. And refusing food was another thing; but she had taken his tray into him just the same and helped where possible, cutting his chicken into bite-sized pieces and leaving him to fend for himself, which had seemed to work. As had her unflappable approach.

'Is there anything you'd like to eat?' she'd asked when he had thrown the menu down furiously without choosing for the following day.

'A large steak—and some French fried potatoes and a dish of sweetcorn and salad—a green one: a very cool, crisp green salad. Impossible, I know, in here.'

'Not in the least. If you don't mind my chopping it up a bit. Not too sure about the steak, though. Maybe we'll have to wait a bit for that. French fries? Why not? You could at least eat them with your fingers.'

How had she been able to shut everything else out while she'd been with him? Dr Patterson, making his round at five o'clock and finding a much more relaxed problem patient, had obviously been impressed, as he'd given her the suspicion of a wink and a raised eyebrow while he'd talked to Mike. But neither of them had mentioned Sarah. It was all part of the hospital routine, getting patients used to accepting administrations, however unpleasant, as part of their recovery. But Mike was no ordinary patient. He felt an intolerable resentment against the necessity to keep still and confined to one room. His only sign of resignation where she was concerned had been as she'd left.

'You'll be on duty again tomorrow, I guess?'

'Yes,' she'd told him quietly, putting magazines where he could reach them with the switch of the remote-control for the television set she had borrowed from another room. At least for tonight he might not be quite so bored. His restlessness could be understood. He was fighting his immobility, not knowing how long before he would be back on his feet, literally.

For his type of man it was the worst punishment. She wanted desperately to help him.

Sister and Nurse Williams were about to go for their meal, leaving a junior nurse on duty with Sarah until they returned. She already knew about the other patients but it was a little different being wholly in charge. Today she had been concentrating on Mike Rayner, but after this he must be integrated with her other duties towards them too.

Sister was smiling at her while her observant eyes were assessing this girl who was undergoing such emotional happenings. 'I hear you've worked a miracle in there,' she commented. 'Think it will last?'

'I hope so. Is all well with these other patients?'

'They are, as you know, having surgery tomorrow. Dr Patterson has seen them this evening and the anaesthetist will be up to see them shortly. Nurse Williams will be back in time for you to go off duty. Goodnight, Nurse.'

'Goodnight, Sister.'

The girl in ward four had come in from one of the ranches, having fallen or been thrown from her horse. Quite apart from a fractured cheekbone she had a fracture of the elbow, so swollen it was unrecognisable, and the X-rays showed fragmentation. She was on Neil Patterson's list and would be on traction splint until they were sure the reduction held, before going into plaster. She also had two cracked ribs and was feeling very unhappy and low, even though she was under some sedation.

Now she was aware of Sarah beside her bed holding her wrist and looking down at her sympathetically.

'Hello, Jenny. I'm Nurse Hillier. Do you need anything? Don't try to talk. Your parents came but you were asleep. They will be here again tomorrow.'

'My—horse?'

'He's fine. Your father asked us to tell you that.'

The door opened and a doctor Sarah hadn't seen before came up to the bed.

'Hi there. I'm Dr Burton. Anaesthetist.' He looked down at the girl in the bed. 'I shall be looking after you tomorrow when you have your op. OK? Jenny, isn't it? Just let me read through your notes, then I'll tell you what we're going to do. Don't worry. You're going to be fine.'

Sarah left them together, while she went to check on the woman patient next door, in for a laminectomy and fusion, which she already knew was removal of a ruptured disc which the X-rays showed to be pressing on the spinal nerve roots, and bone grafting, and could be extremely tricky. Dr Patterson would be doing that one tomorrow.

Heather Wilson was lying flat on her back and obviously feeling very apprehensive. There was too much time to think when one was in a room by oneself and the next day loomed inescapably, filling one's thoughts.

Besides which she was hot and uncomfortable and very relieved to see Sarah.

Every bodily function was agony, but was sometimes necessary. This was real down-to-earth nursing as Sarah's cool hands helped to make her more comfortable, gently slipping her nylon nightdress over her head and another, cooler cotton one in its place.

'Oh—that's better. Thank you,' Heather said gratefully. 'I was so hot.'

'Cotton is much better while you have to stay in bed. Perhaps you could have some brought in tomorrow.'

'Oh—I will. I do possess cotton ones. I guess I wanted to look a bit more glamorous.'

'Well, you look extremely fresh and nice in that one. Oh—here's Dr Burton to tell you all about your op. I'll come back again later.'

Next there was a skin graft, also on Dr Patterson's list. A woman of around fifty and she, at the moment, was quite comfortable, if apprehensive, and reading, her bedside lamp shedding a soft glow.

'Hello, Mrs Garner. Just popped in to see if you wanted anything. You're immersed in your book, I see.'

'Well—it helps take your mind off things,' she replied. 'I just hope I'm going to be OK.'

'Oh, yes, Doctor thinks it will be quite straight-forward. Just a bit uncomfortable for a time. A skin graft is a bit different because its taken from a donor site. Your thigh, I believe, in your case.'

'Mmm. Never expected to have a bit of my thigh sitting on my upper arm,' she mused, trying to be brave. 'I never heard of these things before. What I have. . .'

'A melanoma?'

'Yes. It's cancerous, isn't it?'

Sarah nodded. 'Yes. Yes, it is. But because it's still in the early stages, it should be quite successful.'

'I knew it was serious, you know. Being curious, I asked Dr Patterson right out, after he'd told me I had to have surgery on my arm. I said, "Should I be worried about this, Doctor?" And he said, "Well—it could be rather nasty. We have to remove it at once, and graft new skin over it." So I told him to get on with it, then.'

'Good for you. And this time tomorrow it will be all over. You can go to your bathroom on your own, can't you? Is there anything else you need?'

'No, Nurse. Are you going off duty now?'

'Yes. Quite soon. Your anaesthetist will be seeing you now. So have a good night. See you tomorrow. Just ring your bell if you need anything. Goodnight.'

Nurse Williams was back on duty and Sarah was free to go.

CHAPTER FOUR

IT WAS warmer this evening and Sarah wore just a
light jacket over her beige trousers, a leather bag slung
over one shoulder. The sun's rays caught her hair,
turning it a golden bronze instead of brown and, as
Neil Patterson opened the car door, her perfume—
freshly applied as she had changed from her uniform—
made her, for him, into a very elusive and attractive
woman. He appreciated good taste and liked women
to have an elusive quality, but he hadn't thought of
Sarah in that context—until now, realising with something of a shock that this girl was having a tremendous
impact on him. Until now he had been involved
because he had been the one who had contacted her in
England. And this he need not strictly have done at
all. Since then he had felt very sorry for her, admiring
the courage and strength of character with which she
had accepted the inevitable. Now, as he sank into the
bucket-seat of his Cougar, he smiled wryly, with a hint
of amusement, which fortunately Sarah didn't see. Pity,
he was telling himself, was supposed to be akin to love.
So what? Certainly his senses were alive to the trend,
but it was all rather unexpected nevertheless.

They didn't speak much as he turned away from the
maze of streets towards the suburbs. Tall skyscrapers
rose heavenwards from the city and spread out of it,
stretching away to the east. Sarah saw boats in the
marina, gaily painted now for the short summer
months. Everywhere the trees and shrubs looked green
after the rain. Along the shores tall dark spruce, lodge-
pole pines and cedars lined the beaches, dwarfed by
the slumbering mountains.

He saw her looking at them.

'Up there is Lion's Mountain, Sarah. Supposed to look like two lions guarding the city, if you can stretch your imagination a little.'

'Yes. I read about those—it's a fascinating city. It grows on one.' She didn't really want to talk.

He went on, 'Well, of course, you haven't been able to see anything of it yet. The weather will soon be warmer: we're into May next week. You can see the Capilano suspension bridge in a moment. You should really get in some sightseeing while you are here, Sarah. Which, incidentally, is one of my favourite names.' He was willing her to converse.

'I think it's a family name because both my grandmothers had it too—one was Sarah-Jane, like me, the other Sarah-Elizabeth and my mother too.' She caught her breath. . .her eyes were brimming over. She heard him telling her that he was glad that she wanted to talk about her parents.

'Sometimes people shut off,' he went on, 'because others avoid bringing them into the conversation, mistakenly thinking it will cause more emotion, but when my father died I wanted to talk about him. So did my mother. He was still part of our lives, after all.'

'There are so many happy memories. I don't ever want to forget those,' she whispered.

'There's no reason why you should,' he said firmly as he turned into the Sutcliffes' driveway and leaned across to open the door for her. 'I won't come in. I have a few people coming for drinks later and I *should* get there first.'

'It *is* out of your way, isn't it?'

'Not too much. I enjoyed it. But before you go. . .' as she made a move to get out of the car '. . .would you like to go out for a meal some time, Sarah?'

She looked at him quickly, a little shaken. 'Oh—I don't think. . .'

'What don't you think? Unless, of course, you would rather not. I will understand.'

'It isn't that, Dr Patterson, it's just that. . .'

'It will be a break from the hospital routine for both of us. I'll look forward to it. Perhaps in a week or so. . .'

He revved up the powerful engine and was gone, while she went up the steps feeling bemused by so many things, but the disturbing factor was her awareness of him as a man when he had leaned across to open the car door.

As she crossed the hall, Andrea's voice called out from the kitchen. 'I'm in here, Sarah. Who brought you home? I heard the car, or did you get a cab? Sit down, honey. I'll get you a martini or, better still—my hands are floury—pour us both one. It's in the fridge—and the lemons.'

'It was Dr Patterson.'

'Really?'

'Mmm. He doesn't live this way at all, does he?'

'No. Down by the river, overlooking the marina actually.'

'He's asked me out one evening for a meal.'

'Has he, now? Where is he taking you?'

'He didn't say. And I didn't actually accept. Not for a week or two, obviously.'

'You should go. It will help the days along, having something to look forward to. I know he admires you very much. And you have to start somewhere.'

'He's just being kind, I think.'

'Oh, don't you underestimate yourself, honey. There's more to it than that, knowing how choosy he is about who he takes out. And why not? You're a lovely girl. He isn't missing up a chance; you might be doing a disappearing act on him, if they suddenly want you back in England.'

'No—it isn't like that. I've told him that I'll see Mike Rayner through until he doesn't need extra care.'

'I see. So—how is your problem patient?'

'Not eating enough to keep a sparrow alive, and still as obstinate as ever.'

'Glad to see you?'

'Oh, yes. He welcomed me with open arms. Well— almost. I feel so sorry for him and I mustn't; it's fatal in our profession. It happens all the time, though.'

'Of course it does. You wouldn't have chosen it in the beginning if you hadn't a feeling for sick people. As Charles says, they come and they go and some leave you with the good feeling of another life perhaps saved, or a cure which is satisfying, while others—well, you know, don't you? One has to get the whole thing into the right perspective, and you mustn't bring it home with you.'

'That's right. And in the busy hospitals one is often saying goodbye to a patient while the next is already in his bed. It's the successes, of course, which make it all worthwhile.'

'Sure. Supper won't be long. Do you want to shower, Sarah?'

'Yes, I think so, please.'

She went upstairs as Dr Sutcliffe's key turned in the lock.

Until this evening she hadn't been very sure about anything. Now she was—well, almost. Dr Patterson had struck the right note. She must continue with her work in spite of everything. It gave a purpose to each day. The counselling she had given to others—relatives and patients—was now directed towards herself.

Besides, there was more than one reason for wanting to stay in Canada; at least, for a time.

The next three days were ones in which all the patients, including Mike, needed very careful nursing and all Sarah's skills were stretched going from one room to the next, in spite of the fact that Sister came to help whenever she could, quite apart from the responsibilities which fell to her through administration. Sarah now felt completely integrated. Sister realised what an excellent nurse Sarah was, and told her so. She also told Dr Patterson.

'She is a great asset. And what courage! The patients like her. She has exactly the right manner.'

'She is still under stress, though, even if she hides it so well.'

'Oh, I know. . .'

Sarah, about to leave ward two, had heard every word. Her eyes filled with quick tears, dashed away at once.

So he understood, he knew all the time. Even knowing that seemed to help a great deal. She hadn't realised how much, until that moment. Even though life had to go on—and there was a constant ache in her heart and a sadness which sometimes exhausted her—there was still a strength of will which came through it all; and her work, as every nurse knew, was giving out, helping and caring for real people who needed you. And to be needed, and being there to help brought its own reward.

When Sarah awoke on the morning of the funeral she knew it was going to be one of the worst days of her life. All her strength was called for when she drove behind her father to the tiny church. Dr Sutcliffe and his wife had insisted on going with her and she was even more surprised to see the tall figure in a dark suit waiting at the church door for them. She hadn't thought Dr Patterson would be there too. His presence gave her strength, even though he had to go back to the hospital immediately afterwards.

Her, 'Thank you. . .' came from her heart.

The Sutcliffes were so supportive, driving her back to their house afterwards, not attempting to stop the inevitable summing-up which had to come. All those letters from England too. But they also drew her back to the present.

'Your rancher—how is he making out? Something of a challenge there for you, Sarah,' Dr Sutcliffe observed, watching her reactions.

'Yes. But it's something I feel I have to do. Try to make up for what has happened. Get him mobile again. And along with all the hospital back-up—we will.'

'Good girl. Now—I have to go back to see a patient but——'

'Dr Sutcliffe. . .do you mind if I come with you?'

'If you feel up to it, Sarah. Of course.'

She knew that he and his wife were surprised. But it was something she had to do. She ran upstairs to wash away the traces of tears on her face; be quite alone for a few minutes; gather strength. When she came down she had changed into a silk blouse and cream skirt with a rust sweater. It was a brave effort. Dr Sutcliffe got up from his chair. 'Come along, then, Sarah—it's back to work for us both; if you're sure you feel up to it.' He held her raincoat for her.

'I'm quite sure,' she said, a new note in her voice as she went with him out into the misty afternoon. The rain-washed yellow daffodils and tulips were a sharp reminder, but she closed her mind against the misery in her heart. She couldn't wait to get back to the now familiar hospital environment. She needed the routine and responsibility her job entailed, working among others who understood the same commitments as she did herself and she was sure it was what her father would have wanted too.

She looked pale and strained but the resolve was there as well. Sarah was on duty, and for as long as she wanted to stay. She drew a deep breath and made her way back to ward six. Mike Rayner had a visitor. She saw a stetson hat lying on the chair and the burly weathered-faced man who got up from beside the bed gave her a slow grin. 'Hi, there.'

'This,' Mike said slowly, and she saw that he looked tired, 'is the special nurse—I told you about her, Joe.'

'Lucky guy,' Joe teased. 'You've been holding out on me. Maybe I can come in for a rest some time. I guess I'll be off now—get back on the road. Anything you need, Mike, just give us a buzz.'

'Nothing. Unless you can supply a new pair of these, Joe!'

'Wish I could. But don't worry about things up at the ranch. I won't let anything slide. You've got yourself some good guys up there. Midge sends her regards. Says you're to get back up there soon. Guess she's hand-rearing one of the calves. Calls her April. A rare one for newborn calves is Midge. She'll rear it.'

'OK. Now get those papers in the post, Joe. And——'

'I know. Keep the stock rolling.'

'The beef stock, Joe. While the price is right.'

'OK, boss.'

Sarah busied herself at the treatment table, still trying to absorb the stark reality of her loss. She didn't feel like making conversation. Indeed, it was Mike who broke the silence after watching her surreptitiously for a few moments.

'Why didn't you tell me, Sarah? I'm more than sorry.'

She refused to let the welling tears escape. But he had seen.

'Shouldn't you be off duty?'

'No. I—prefer to be here. Your sheet is wrinkled and those pillows need something done to them.'

'Don't fuss. . .' he ground out irritably. 'The whole thing is one hell of a mess. I feel inadequate in this situation and I'm hating every minute of it.'

His blue eyes fixed on hers defiantly. The fight was there but the strength to cope was not. She felt sorry for him again. Slipping the thermometer into his grimly protesting mouth, having noticed signs of a raised temperature, she wondered if it was because of his

visitor or a slight infection. Either way, it was something they could do without in his present state.

Later, when she had made his bed comfortable and
settled him back on his pillows and adjusted his pulley
straps, he told her that she was quite a nurse. 'Joe
thinks so too.'

'I know. I heard you.'

The phone in the corner bleeped. The operator was
putting a call through for him. It was a woman, her
Canadian accent a slow drawl.

'Is that Mike Rayner's room?'

'Yes, it is. Who is speaking please?'

'Can't he talk himself? It's Monique.'

'Yes, he can. I'll give him the phone. Hold on.'

'Say—who are you? The nurse?'

'Yes.'

'You sound very English. Are you?'

'Yes. Just one moment.'

Mike, who had been listening with raised eyebrows,
reached for the receiver with his good hand, mouthing,
'Who?'

'It's Monique,' she told him as he took it, and she
saw his face lighten.

'Hi, there.' Then, 'Yes. I guess so. You finally got to
me, then.' He looked a little angry now. Sarah made
for the door.

Collecting some more medication and fresh towels
and tissues, she remembered that he was low on
oranges. With her arms full, she was just about to put
these on the chair outside of his door when she heard
him still on the phone. Hesitating before going in, she
decided to wait, gratefully sitting down. He sounded
agitated; this roused her nursing instincts at once. It
was the last thing she wanted. But it was obviously
personal.

'For God's sake, Monique—it was you who hung
up.' Then, 'Yes—I did. OK—so you don't like hospitals; what's that supposed to mean?' Silence, while

Sarah accepted that she was eavesdropping, but the brooding disappointment in his voice was only adding to the pain and frustration, pressures he could do without right now. 'OK—so you're not driving down here—I heard you. No—forget it. . .' He sounded angry as he went on, 'What the hell did you expect? At least—you might have come to see for yourself. Typical, isn't it, Monique? No—don't bother.'

Sarah heard the phone slammed down into its cradle.

She went quietly into his room.

'Are you all right, Mike?'

He didn't answer, staring with his head turned away out of the window at a sky angrily coloured with red and yellow streaks among the darkening clouds moving swiftly towards the mountains. It seemed the elements were angry in keeping with his mood, she thought wryly.

When she went to fetch in the clean towels she had left on the chair outside she left a message for Dr Patterson when he was free before going back in. Mike was still agitated and she insisted on taking his temperature. It was three points above an earlier reading and his BP was also swinging in the same direction, and there were beads of perspiration on his forehead.

She decided to bring his bed-wash forward. He was a fanatic about personal freshness and accepted a wash with warm water and a clean cotton top. There were beads of perspiration on his chest, making the fair hair cling damply. He still looked morose and as though he was hating submitting to the ordeal.

'You can finish the rest yourself if you can manage it,' she said because he hadn't spoken at all. 'Everything is to hand. Feeling cooler now?'

'I—wouldn't say that.' But relief that he was to have a hand in it showed through. Tactfully she moved out of range, leaving the curtains drawn, but she heard his muffled oath of annoyance when he discovered it was not so easy to cope for himself.

When she was clearing everything away and he insisted on attempting to brush his own hair, leaving it more tousled than before, she quietly took the brush and did it for him.

'Dr Patterson. . .' he said suddenly '. . .he's not very old for a surgeon, is he?'

She said tactfully, 'He's very clever. I expect he made it early on. I like him very much. He's splendid to work with.' She saw that he was pressing his hand to his forehead; the X-rays had shown no contusions but there could be bruising, and there was his raised BP too.

'It's probably tension, Mike. Are you worried about what's happening at the ranch?'

'Sure, I'm worried. I should be up there. Do you have any idea how much needs doing now? Branding beef cattle to be graded for the market. A go-ahead plan for the year to be got underway. Competition is on the increase with beef cattle—— Oh, it's no use—this head.'

'I could give you something, but I'd rather Dr Patterson did. You've got a good stockman—leave it all to him for a while.'

'Oh, sure. Joe's fine. But I'm the one who makes the decisions. I like it that way. So do they. I've reared that herd; I know every head out on the range. I've ridden out last winter with snow higher than they were and got them back in; not lost one. I don't know what to do when I'm not there with my finger on the trigger, as it were. That seem strange to you?'

'No. Not at all. But you have to stop worrying.'

Neil Patterson opened the door and came up to the bed, his observant eyes taking everything in in a glance, especially his patient's dewy eyes, heavy with slight feverishness.

'How are you?' he asked, reaching for the chart which Sarah handed him, not giving away the fact that she had called him.

'Except for a headache I guess I'm OK,' he said stubbornly.

'Been getting steamed up today?'

Sarah remembered the phone call and a woman named Monique. Yes. That was when it had started.

'I guess so. Would that do it?'

'It might. Or an infection somewhere. I wouldn't have thought so, though. We'll keep an eye on it. I don't want to introduce more antibiotics at this stage unless I have to, so I suggest you keep quiet and leave any problems to someone else for the time being. We'll get those sutures taken out tomorrow, I think.'

He handed Sarah back the chart, then looked carefully at Mike's face beneath the golden stubble of beard. 'I don't think there should be too much scarring, you know. It will take time, of course.'

'I don't have the time to sit around and wait for that,' Mike ground out. 'I'm not concerned with my face, Dr Patterson, it's these—and this. . .' He surveyed his raised plasters and pointed to his right arm. 'How long before this becomes operative?'

'Two months perhaps.'

'So when will I leave here?'

'Probably in six to eight weeks. No promises, Mike. But, barring complications——'

'I'll make it in four.'

'OK, Mike, it's your life,' Dr Patterson told him decisively, 'but if you don't get those bones setting properly and the muscles healed before you attempt to get back to work, it could take even longer. You did get rather smashed up, you know—only days ago. There are some rather intricate repairs going on under that plaster. It took me over five hours to make a good job of you; don't undo it, there's a good guy.' He looked across the bed at Sarah, at her pallor and dark-rimmed eyes. 'Could you ask Sister Gadd to take over now, Nurse Hillier? It's time you weren't here.'

'I don't need any nurse around,' Mike broke in, sweating a little with rising temper.

'I'll be in first thing in the morning. Give in gracefully—we all have to some time or other. It's easier in the end,' the doctor finished.

Sarah followed him to the door.

He turned to her, his voice low, 'You shouldn't still be here, you know,' he said seriously. 'He's fine. Go off now, Sarah. Those are orders.'

Sarah promised that she would do that. The warmth and kindness in the new friends she had made in Canada were heart-warming, something she would never be able to forget, especially in the future.

Sarah had been relieved to be able to get away early, and because she hadn't been expected at the hospital at all the other patients were covered and Sister Gadd on duty. 'The dragon' some called her, but she was always in complete control and Sarah liked her and had great respect for her. She wasn't unlike Sister Maine. How long ago all that seemed now, she thought, sitting in the yellow cab nosing its way out of the hospital gates.

When she arrived back Andrea was busy as usual in the kitchen where she loved to be and sent Sarah up for a shower or bath before her husband arrived home.

'Dinner is at seven, honey, so you have plenty of time to relax and unwind this evening. No need to change. I love that blouse and skirt. Why do English clothes have that certain something about them?'

'This does happen to be made in Britain,' Sarah commented, 'but believe me, most these days seem to be made in Taiwan or Hong Kong. I have to admit, some of them are beautifully made too, and usually much cheaper.'

'It's like that over here too,' Andrea agreed. 'It's really good to have another woman around to talk to about ordinary things like clothes and fashion. My wonderful husband isn't the least bit interested in what I wear, as long as it's right, of course.'

Sarah, going upstairs, knew why Andrea was talking about ordinary things, like clothes, and hoped she would be able to go along with it for the rest of the evening. She was glad that she had gone into the hospital that afternoon. Perhaps each day would make the sadness in her heart a little less, now that all she had left of her father were her memories. Even these would fade in time. Now she had to get on with her own life. And that was under wraps at present.

Dr Patterson's last appointment had been at five p.m. A little before six he left quickly and drove out of the hospital gates, turning in the direction of the Sutcliffes' home. Sarah hadn't known he was coming, looking up in surprise from some documents she was going through when Andrea brought him into the lounge.

She got up. 'Oh—Dr Patterson—I. . .'

'Sit down, Sarah. We're not at the hospital now. I've been invited to supper. You didn't know?'

Andrea broke in. 'I thought I'd keep it a surprise, Neil. Charles is changing—he'll be down in a minute. What will you drink? Sherry? Scotch? Vermouth?'

'Sherry for me, thanks, Andrea.'

Because Sarah had barely touched hers he picked up her glass and handed it to her. 'Doctor's orders—drink it and have another. My father used to say it's the best tonic in the world.'

'Really? Was he a doctor too?'

'He was. A very clever one. He died two years ago. A massive coronary.'

'Oh—I'm so sorry.' He recognised the pain in her voice. She truly meant it.

'It was a good way for him to go—but not for my mother, of course. She lives on Victoria Island; my brother and his family are close by, so I know she's OK and not too lonely. I get over there occasionally,

but she's a very busy lady, my mother—and I have to
fit in my visits between her many social and lame-dog
activities. Ah—how are you, Charles? I hear you've
done big things today.'

'Oh—the grapevine spreads rapidly. Hi there, Neil.
So, what did you hear?'

Sarah got up then and left them to themselves, while
she seemed to be doing everything in limbo. Even the
salads she carried to the table for Andrea, and the
sizzling T-bone steaks from under the grill, did nothing
to bring back reality. Andrea let her help, understanding that to do things, anything, was the only way out
for her immediately.

She barely touched her meal, listening to the drone
of conversation around her, grateful that they didn't
force her into it. But after three cups of coffee and
some brandy she knew the day's events were hitting
home and had to be reckoned with.

When Dr Sutcliffe and his other guest were talking
quietly about microvascular surgery, in which at any
other time she would have been silently interested,
Sarah got up, unnoticed, and left them. Only Andrea
followed her into the hall.

'Do you want to go to bed, honey?' she asked
solicitously.

'I think so. Do you mind?'

'Of course not. I'll say goodnight for you. They'll
understand. Try to get some sleep. And don't go in
tomorrow if you're not up to it.'

'I will be,' she said stoically, and meant it.

Meanwhile, Mike, waiting for Sarah next morning,
was becoming irritated by Sister Gadd's insistence that
one of the other nurses must get on with his washing,
at least until Sarah took over. Actually she was in the
building, but was having to get some forms signed by
Administration before sending them back to the
authorities.

Since Mike was complaining of a shooting pain in his

left leg, Sister put a request through to Neil for him to visit. As soon as he walked in, the patient asked angrily, 'Did you put a pin through this one?' He positively glared at the doctor.

'Two, actually, Mike.'

'Then that's it. Something's wrong. Just what it feels like.'

'I wouldn't have thought so, but we'll get a picture done. It could be some nerve pressure. Much more likely. Meanwhile, rest it——'

'As if I can do anything else.'

'Have you had your jab?'

'Not since very early.'

'Right. Perhaps more medication. I don't want to disturb the plaster at this stage unless I have to, so we'll try that first.'

'Where is Nurse Hillier?'

'She'll be in later. She had business to attend to.'

'And yesterday?'

Neil told him as carefully as he could about her father's funeral. A spasm crossed Mike's face. It could have been for his own pain, or hers. Neil added, 'Your face looks much improved—that should cheer you up a bit—and I see you've acquired a beard. I wouldn't mind attempting to grow one myself, though quite honestly I'm not the type to suit it, am I?'

There was no answer from his patient: he was watching the door for Sarah to come through.

Sarah was helping Sister with Heather Wilson. It was imperative that she be turned properly and the alignment of the spine maintained. There were some problems with the patient's urinary output and Sister thought she should be catheterised.

'Will you see to it, Nurse Hillier?'

'Yes, Sister.' She explained to Heather what she was about to do, and why. 'It may only be for a day or two.' The lower limbs were then checked for mobility and the wound checked to ensure that there were no leakages. This too Sarah explained as she went along, calling the junior nurse to help her with making her comfortable.

'Glad it's all over, Heather?'

'Oh, yes, Nurse. I was really scared.'

'I know. But Dr Patterson looked after you. You couldn't have anyone better than him.'

'He was marvellous. I guess I'm not going to feel very comfortable though for quite a while.'

'We'll see how you go. Sometimes you can sit out of bed after a few days.'

The other patients were asleep. Jenny was still under sedation, and Mrs Garner had also been given strong painkillers, for the donor site on her upper thigh was even more painful than the actual graft and surgery on her upper arm.

Leaving Nurse Williams—who had returned from her break—to supervise, Sarah went into ward number six where Mike was growing more impatient by the minute.

'You could have rung the bell. It's right here,' she told him, looking straight into his eyes.

'I thought you were assigned to me, whereas you're never here when you're wanted.'

'Not exclusively, Mike, but for most of the time, yes. What's wrong?'

When he ground out between clenched teeth that he needed a bedpan, she was immediately professional and drew the curtains around his bed.

'I'll be back in a few minutes,' she said quietly, going into the corridor after closing the door.

Debby, coming along with a basket of medication from the pharmacy, stopped to say hello and ask how she was coping before going around the corridor to her own section. 'May see you at lunch. . .' she called over her shoulder.

'Maybe.' Just then nothing was further from Sarah's mind, as she opened the door of ward six and went to administer to her patient, her help being accepted so sulkily that she asked if there had been any more of the shooting pains in his leg.

'No.'

'Then it was probably just a one-off, as Dr Patterson suspected.'

'Oh—he's bound to be right. . .'

'He usually is,' she said lightly.

CHAPTER FIVE

AT LAST Sarah was off duty and free to go. It was two days later, and all her patients were showing signs of recovery. But as she passed Jenny's room and heard voices she remembered that her parents were coming tonight to talk to Dr Patterson.

As she reached the swing doors, he came from Jenny's room and, seeing her ahead, called her name.

Her heart jumped. She drew a deep breath and waited. This was getting ridiculous. She was behaving like an adolescent.

When he reached her he asked if she was ready to leave.

'Almost. You've been seeing Jenny's parents? How are they taking it now?'

He fell into step beside her, both heading for the lift. 'Still shocked at her facial injuries. To them she looks unrecognisable of course, but I've assured them that the swelling and discoloration will fade and the sutures will be removed in five or six days.' He glanced at her as they went into the lift. 'I can take you back if you will hang on for about ten minutes. Unless you have transport, Sarah.'

'No, but——'

'Ten minutes at the outside.' He left her on the next floor down, touching her shoulder with a gentle pressure, but she was very aware of it as the doors slid together and she went on down to the ground floor and the nurses' changing-rooms.

Slipping out of her uniform, she crossed to the washbasins and freshened up, applying a touch of lipstick and a light foundation. This evening her eyes

were more grey than green, looking back at her speculatively from the mirror, large tonight because she was
tired, but still sensitively aware. And she was conscious
of a slight nervousness too. But why? Neil Patterson
had offered her a lift, but he didn't have to, which must
surely mean that he wanted to. But one was never
quite sure with him, she decided as she brushed her
hair vigorously into a shining cloud around her face,
releasing her inner tensions at the same time. She
didn't know very much about him, his background
away from the hospital, but he obviously hadn't anyone
special to meet this evening.

And Neil, scrubbing under the shower, could no
longer deny the effect which Sarah was having on his
masculinity. He wanted to be with her. It was there,
showing all the signs, and he certainly hadn't felt like
this about any other woman since Rachel, with whom
he had his only really serious relationship. He still
thought about her sometimes.

It had been during their early days at university.
They had fallen in love and it had lasted right the way
through the years until graduation and medical school,
becoming less powerful, it was true, but they had still
been so close. He hadn't envisaged ever being without
her, but she had had other plans, namely a post in a
teaching hospital in Australia, and she hadn't even told
him that she had applied.

Neil had been deeply hurt, rejection hard to take,
and he had missed her. She had left a gap in his life.
But he had accepted that it was finally over and, since
then, no liaison had been allowed to become too
serious.

He had been one of the lucky ones to get into a
teaching hospital and, six months on the wards later,
was junior house surgeon; eventually he had come here
to this hospital as a senior house surgeon.

He had earned his reputation and was proud of it—
his friends too—and his independence, but now he was

very aware of his feelings for Sarah. Maybe he should back off before he got in too deeply.

Except that he felt the need to protect her in some way, the protectiveness of the male towards the female. Primitive it might be, but it was what he was feeling.

He brushed his hair into place, grabbed his briefcase and made for the door. She had been waiting quite long enough.

She looked so feminine, standing there in her beige skirt and cream silk blouse, suddenly very special. He hurried towards her, smiling, and Sarah, very aware of his freshness, his hair still damp from his shower, felt a glow of anticipation as she smiled back and walked beside him to where his car was parked. Once she was in her seat the car nosed out into the traffic and both were silent, but it was a nice companionable silence.

Neil was turning something over in his mind, then decided to come right out with it.

'I—would very much like to take you for a meal one evening, Sarah, as I said. Would Thursday be OK? Provided you want to, of course.'

She thought for a moment. 'Yes. I'd like it very much. And Thursday will be fine. I'm off duty at six-thirty.'

'Shall I pick you up around seven-thirty, then, or eight?'

'Eight perhaps might be safer. Just in case of an emergency.'

'Right. Eight, then.'

Her heart was beating a little faster, especially when he gave her another quick delighted smile before concentrating once more on the highway packed with coaches and cars, all waiting at the traffic lights, before surging forward again.

But they reached the Sutcliffes' home fairly quickly and she got out at once.

'Thanks again,' she said sincerely.

'It's my pleasure, Sarah,' he told her, and meant it.

There were letters from England, from nurses on her ward and others in the hospital. From Sister Maine, from her neighbours and from Mr Attwood, with forms for her signature.

No way could one's mind break away because life wasn't like that, she thought; besides, now there was nothing to do but face it all head on, and hope that time would make everything less fraught.

Sarah spent the evening answering her correspondence and it was only just before she went to bed that she remembered to tell Andrea about Neil's invitation.

'Good. I'm glad.' Andrea beamed. 'Nice to look forward to. It's time you broke out of your shell and——'

'Meanwhile,' Dr Sutcliffe put in, 'Andrea and I want you to consider this as your home. We are adamant about that. It's the next best thing to having our daughter around, isn't it, honey?'

'Yes, it is. But I guess we have to wait until July for that to happen.'

'Is she in Canada?'

'New Zealand, I'm afraid. Long way,' Andrea told her. 'Doing research with a team of meds out in the bush. She seems to be enjoying it, though, in spite of the dust and discomfort. That's her latest picture—on the table.'

'Oh—she's very pretty, isn't she?' Sarah had got up to look at a true daughter of her parents. Smiling, and obviously happy, against a backcloth of wooden huts and trees.

'We think so. But then, so are you,' Dr Sutcliffe said unashamedly. 'And to think that I was sitting next to you on that plane for six thousand miles and never made a pass.'

'Charles—behave!' his wife admonished him, but Sarah wasn't deceived. She knew that his teasing was aimed at lifting her mind from the searing tragedy which sometimes snowballed into heartbreak. It was the kind which was so fraught that the mind only absorbed it in small, sudden doses as the hours and days went by. Just when one thought one was coping, stark reality returned again and the tears emerged once more, although now only when Sarah was alone.

Thursday was a very busy and somewhat fraught day at the hospital.

Nurse Williams was doing the later shift so Sarah, with Sister tied to her office for lengthy periods, had much more to do with only a first-year to help.

Mrs Garner had gone home with orders 'not to move that arm around too much' from Dr Patterson. Her leg was still very sore and she would have to rest a great deal for it to heal.

'The sutures from your graft will be taken out after eight days,' Sarah told her. 'There are rather a lot of them and they are very small. But the dressings on the donor site will remain *in situ* for at least twelve days. Maybe longer. Don't worry if it becomes a little hardened, even unpleasant: it will be removed when you have your bath. We'll be seeing you again before that. The worst is over now, Mrs Garner.'

'I—hope so. And that it's been total.'

'We will be keeping a check for quite some time to make sure there is no reoccurence,' Dr Patterson told her finally.

Heather Wilson was allowed out of bed for short periods each day. She also was going in the right direction. Jenny was still recovering only slowly, her face extremely uncomfortable and her other injuries responding to treatment, but she resented all of it very much and was not an easy patient, which was understandable.

She liked Sarah, though, and this helped a lot.

Mike Rayner was different, very demanding and resentful still, and later that morning, as Sarah administered to him, she had difficulty coping with him. But he was also her special patient. His need and trust in her, to which he wouldn't admit, was enough.

As his nurse she was privileged. She understood, without questions, what was going on in his body whose weakness he cursed daily. But now he also knew that even she couldn't predict whether or not he would ever again be the same hard-muscled, hard-riding cowboy who thought nothing of a whole day in the saddle, who could throw a rope with sure success to catch an errant steer, or hold one for branding, putting his strength against the animal which would grow into a heavy beef yield. And how would his legs take to tight-fitting leather boots? And suppose he did make the saddle, and got thrown—undoing all this knitting together of bones and tissues and muscles——

'Oh—hell. . .' he groaned, forgetting Sarah's sitting at the table writing up her report notes on his chart.

She made no move to go to the bed apart from looking up, guessing the reason for his outburst. But after a time she suggested that he might like his bed moved to face the window.

'You can at least see the buildings and mountain-tops, instead of only the wall and the door.'

'OK. When do we get on to it?'

'Now if you like. Hold tight—your bed is on wheels anyway.'

When he was turned in the new direction she added, 'I'll open this door on to the balcony. Don't know why we didn't think of it before. Maybe you can be pushed out there for a while.'

'That would be a step in the right direction. When?'

'When what?'

'When do you get to ask him—if we have to?'

'Dr Patterson's operating until early afternoon; when he comes round later perhaps, or tonight—I'll suggest it then.'

She stopped, seeing the quick movement as he

turned his head. He raised his eyebrows. 'You see
him—away from the hospital?'

'Yes. He sometimes drives me back to Dr Sutcliffe's
house. I'm staying with them.'

'I didn't realise you moved in such high circles—or
on that level socially,' he said coldly. 'Is Dr Patterson
the reason you are staying over here?' There was an
imperative note in his voice, demanding an answer.

Sarah didn't reply at once as she stood looking out
of the window at the sun glinting on the snowy peaks
above the skyscraper buildings.

When Sarah returned from her own lunch looking
crisp and fresh in her uniform, Monique was in room
six. Because there was no sound of voices from within
she had thought he was alone, but the girl was at the
window, turning quickly at the sound of the door
opening. Her vibrant, even flamboyant personality
seemed to fill the room.

There was an explosive atmosphere and Sarah felt
intrusive as she backed towards the door, apologising.
'I'm so sorry—I thought you were alone. . .' She
looked at Mike's visitor. 'Would you like some
coffee—or tea, or something? It won't take a minute,'
she asked, meeting the flashing dark eyes in an effort
to make her stay, because she had already picked up
her bag and Sarah, having summed up the situation,
knew she couldn't let her leave this way. It wouldn't
help her patient at all.

The long black hair reaching to her shoulders was
tossed back with a quick movement; the way, Sarah's
brain recorded, this girl seemed to do most things.

'There's no point in my staying any longer, thanks.
Besides, I have some things to do in town. Hospitals
give me the creeps anyway.'

Sarah tactfully withdrew, but she couldn't help over-
hearing her next remark.

'Well—it certainly doesn't look as if you'll be back
at the ranch for ages yet; as I've said, Mike, someone

needs to keep an eye on those guys up there, even if
they do object.'

'Stay away, Monique.' Mike's voice was angry,
deadly. 'Joe won't brook any interference—he's doing
a good job and that goes for the other hands. They
know the way I have that ranch run. And it's not going
to be turned into a dude ranch, not this year. That's
final.'

The door opened and the girl in close-fitting white
trousers and green shirt blouse stamped out—no other
word for it—and slammed the door, ignoring Sarah
who was putting away the clean sheets she had brought
with her.

'How dare she?' It was out before she knew it. And,
going in to Mike, she asked, 'Doesn't your friend
realise this is a hospital?'

'I doubt it,' he said morosely from the bed. 'Monique
is a law unto herself. She's a damned good business-
woman, but on her own terms. She has no right,
though, to go upsetting the guys up there, or try to run
my ranch. We're not married yet. . .'

'Are you engaged, then, Mike?'

'I guess so. In a way.' He shifted a little, grimacing
as he tried to rest his arm. 'Monique is a great girl. I've
known her since we came out here. We went to the
same school—one room behind the trading post then.
Her folks ran a summer resort—fishing lodge; she's
made it into a trailer park as well and started up a
restaurant. The dude ranch at my place is a good idea
I suppose from a money view.'

'What is a dude ranch?'

'Oh, guests—for the summer. Taking them on trail
rides, camping out—that sort of thing. I've got the
horses but the whole thing needs a lot of organising.
Monique wants to take over that part of it. I guess it
could work out, but when I'm not sure I postpone
decisions. It must wait until I'm back in harness again.
Only Monique has jumped the gun a bit and already

put out feelers for guests and been checking out the horses. The guys won't stand for that and Joe certainly won't. So—now that she has to retract she is a very angry lady.'

'I saw that. And it doesn't do you any good,' she said firmly, 'to have all this pressure. Joe is managing, isn't he?'

'I thought so.'

'Then trust him. I liked him.'

'Yeah. He's a great guy. Been with us ten years or more. Oh—God—I can't just lie here and do nothing,' he burst out despairingly, looking up into the face of the nurse he had to rely on for his medical needs and now for some reassurance.

She pulled up a chair and sat down, meeting the blue eyes she now knew as well as her own. 'You have no choice; you know that. Why not call Joe and have a chat? Put him in the picture. He is probably keeping all this from you because he doesn't want to worry you.'

'I don't want to appear disloyal to Monique in front of the men.'

'You don't have to. Just reiterate your own wishes and leave the rest to him. I'm sure he'll cope.'

'So am I. Will you hand me the phone, please?'

She did so. Then she left the room. Had she said too much? Or had he? It was an explosive situation between two people of very determined aspirations. Yet it wasn't just a lovers' tiff; for she had no doubt that that was what they were, or had been. If it was just that she would not have dreamed of expressing an opinion. Maybe she shouldn't have anyway. But he had asked for it, and she had tried to help. Oh, heavens, if that wasn't patient involvement, then what was it?

And hadn't she felt bitchy towards that girl? she asked herself with a new awareness, and protective towards her patient? Or just sorry for him in his

intolerable circumstances? Either way, she must draw
the line against more involvement in the future. But
she was still puzzled. If they were in love—getting
married some time, which would account for Mike's
being anxious to see her, have her near him—why had
she taken so long? And why did they fight every time?

Sarah had been really looking forward to their night
out, and Neil had chosen a good restaurant—not only
for the food but for the panoramic view—from where
they could look right down over the tops of the
skyscraper buildings to blue waters beyond, on little
moored boats and sandy beaches; on the parkland
away to the left, and the spreading houses on tiers
rising up towards the huge towering mountains. A truly
magnificent view, enhanced by music in the background, and her companion in his formal dark suit
across the table was exciting too. He leaned forward.

'Don't you like my choice of wine, Sarah?'

'Very much.'

'Then drink it. It will help you unwind.'

'I'm not uptight tonight. I want to talk to you, if you
don't mind, about finding somewhere to stay, nearer to
the hospital.'

'OK. We'll talk about it later. Right now I want you
to enjoy the marvellous food they do here. And away
from the hospital my name is Neil—agreed?'

'Oh—yes, of course.' The glimmer of a smile transformed her face, bringing the eyes to life as they met
his when he leaned forward once again to fill her glass.

Tonight she was wearing the only suitable dress she
had brought with her: a classically styled cream silk
jersey, in which she knew she looked good. Neil had
excellent taste himself and appreciated the way Sarah
seemed to fit in with the expensive restaurant he had
chosen to bring her to, a round building with windows
from every viewpoint.

Her expression tonight was still pensive but she

hadn't brought her sadness with her, making an effort to shut off this one emotion from the others. She appreciated that Neil was trying to make her evening with him the beginning of a slow recovery.

Later, he said, 'We'll have more coffee, shall we? Sorry—you were drifting again.' He had reached across to touch her hand, effectively breaking into her thoughts.

It was unexpected, the way she reacted to him then, the corners of her mouth tilting upwards normally. She felt suddenly happy. 'Please!'

He was looking into her eyes. She was responsive, staying with him, everything beginning to seem a little unreal, the scene outside changing as lights sprang up all over the city; neon lights—more than she had ever seen—flashing in the streets and specially towards the downtown area. There was beginning a dream-like quality about being here with this man whose conversation she found stimulating and whom physically she found a little daunting, and she didn't know what he wanted of her.

'Why not come right out with what is bothering you?' he asked. 'I want to help.'

'I know that.'

'So—let's talk. You will have to return to the UK some time, of course.'

Sarah nodded. 'The solicitors want me to go home soon. I will put it off, I think.'

'They're your executors?'

'Yes. Everything was left to me. The house—everything.' She closed her eyes. 'I can't face that part of it yet.'

'That's understandable. Surely it can wait for a while?'

'I think it will have to. We can discuss anything on the telephone if it's urgent.'

His face reflected his concern. 'Do you want my opinion or am I pressurising you?'

'You are going to tell me to stay and get on with my work, aren't you?'

He nodded, watching her revolving the glass in her hand while she sipped her strong black coffee appreciatively from the tiny cup.

'For a time, yes. There will always be more patients, and Mike is over the worst, but if you have to go. . .'

'No—not just yet. Can I wait until I've found somewhere to live first? I simply can't go on occupying Dr Sutcliffe's spare room and accepting his generosity. He won't let me contribute. Besides, I need an apartment of my own to go back to. I still don't know where the shops are. I'd like to do some exploring for myself.'

'That's a splendid idea. Do you want hospital accommodation, or your own room?'

'A small apartment would be fine, I think.'

'Well, that shouldn't be difficult. May I help?'

'I was rather hoping you would.'

'Then I'll call up a few real estate people tomorrow and get you some rental listings, then take you to see them in the evening. You will be free at six and I don't expect to be any later than that myself.'

'Well—thank you,' she said gratefully. 'You've been marvellous, right from the start, and you needn't have been. I was a complete stranger.'

'I don't feel you were ever that. You're also a very attractive lady and once I'd seen you I didn't want to let you go. Still don't. I'm looking after my interests too, you know.'

She wasn't taking him seriously but nothing was that serious any more. The wine had ironed out the final tension creases from her forehead. The unreality of the situation, the décor, the music, gently cocooned her, and his protective manner, as he came to pull back her chair, slipping a hand through her arm as they went towards the lift and down to the foyer, made her easily accept any decision he made. One was that they should drive through the city on the highways and interwoven streets, past the neon signs, down to the water, in contrast looking like fiords—that kind of setting; past the harbour, the bobbing boats and away in the distance. . .

'The Capilano Suspension Bridge,' Neil told her in answer to her query. 'Perhaps, if we can scrounge a full day together, I could take you over to Victoria Island—you really need longer, of course, but you have a lot to see before you slip away again. You will let me show you, won't you, Sarah?'

He parked the car in a layby overlooking the scenery they had passed through, and in the close proximity of the car seats, her shoulder touching his, she knew as his face blurred in the deepening twilight, hesitating, but only for a moment, that he was going to kiss her.

She made no attempt to stop him, wanting it too. His arm slipped around her shoulders and she was drawn to him. At first it was just a gentle pressure of his lips on hers, but suddenly the pressure grew stronger and there was rising passion in his kiss before he finally moved, putting his face against hers.

Sarah couldn't speak. His voice held a tremor. 'I had to do that. You aren't angry?'

'No. Of course not.'

After a few minutes during which his kisses grew stronger, more probing, and her own responses more exciting, she drew away.

'I ought to go now,' she said softly. 'I may be keeping Dr Sutcliffe up. I don't have a key.'

'I didn't think of that. It's been a wonderful evening, Sarah. We must do it again soon.'

He started the car, his hand finding hers on her lap. Little thrusts of happiness crept into her heart at his firm and comforting touch, surprising even herself.

The lights were still on in the hall and Dr Sutcliffe himself opened the door.

'Hi, you two. Do come in, Neil. A nightcap?'

'No, thanks. I'm driving and it's quite late. Thanks

all the same, Charles. Besides, Sarah needs her sleep. See you tomorrow. Goodnight.' And to her, in a different tone which didn't go unnoticed by the doctor, 'I hope you enjoyed it as much as I did, Sarah.'

She apologised for keeping her hosts up, which they both emphatically denied, asking where Neil had taken her and were suitably impressed.

'Dr Sutcliffe, I think I ought to tell you that I'm going apartment-hunting tomorrow evening. Neil is going to help me. I've decided to stay on for a time.'

'Good news,' he said at once. 'About your staying on, I mean. And don't forget, we shall both be here if you need any help or advice. You don't have to rush into anything, but you can't go far wrong with Neil to vet a place for you.' Fortunately for Sarah, she didn't see their raised eyebrows as she went up to her room.

Methodically putting everything ready for the morning, as was her usual way, she slid into bed, stretching her legs down into the cool softness. Tonight she didn't need anything to make her sleep, as she was no longer in limbo. Tonight she held the tip of a challenge in her hands. Neil had given her more than a tentative plan for the next few weeks. He had given her new confidence in herself as a woman. In fact, she could be just a little in love with him. It was the first time she had been kissed since Jeremy. And only a natural shyness had held her back from being even more responsive. So there was a latent excitement in the knowledge that tomorrow evening she was to go out with him again.

CHAPTER SIX

THERE was the inevitable reaction, the sharp truth as to why Sarah was here in Vancouver at all: it brought a rush of tears and she fell asleep while they dried on her face.

But even Mike Rayner noticed the new lightness in her step next day, although his first reaction to her 'Good morning' was, 'You're late. Ten minutes. And you look as if you've been up all night, Nurse Hillier. It won't do. . .' all this delivered in mock serious tones.

'Oh—I see that Mr Rayner is feeling very much better this morning,' she told him. 'As it happens, I had a very good sleep last night, and as for being late, I went to get you some more fruit, since you seem to devour it at such a fast rate—and here is your mail. So you are not neglected in the least, are you?'

'Well, you did say you were going out last night, so I naturally thought——'

'Surely not that I would allow it to interfere with my duties here? Don't you know that a nurse learns to separate the two things completely after the first year?'

'I guess it seemed an interminably long night for some reason.'

'You didn't sleep?'

'Not for long. In any case, I'm an early riser and one tends to keep the same pattern.'

She left him while he tore open the envelope of one of his letters. She guessed it to be from Monique. She checked through the list on her table, giving him time before going to start the day's routine.

He was lying deep in thought, gazing out at the bright morning unseeingly. There were shadows playing on the mountains in the distance. She stood still, watching them, waiting for him: his frown was back.

'You still have another one to open,' she reminded him while she folded his towel.

'So?' He watched as she shook down the thermometer. He was in a stubborn mood. Sarah decided to play it with a firm hand.

'Mike—can we get started, please? Open your mouth.'

He did so, still thoughtful, Something in his letter obviously bothered him. His pulse was unsteady; her cool hand on his wrist sparked off more irritation. 'How much longer do I need this—this "special nursing", as you call it? It's becoming a bore.'

'Would you rather be in a ward with other patients?'

He shook his head. 'I'd rather not be here at all. Will you be off duty this afternoon?' he said as an afterthought.

'No—I shall be working right through because I want to be free early this evening. Dr Patterson is going to help me look for an apartment if I'm to stay over here for a time.'

'I see. So—you're not going back to the UK just yet?'

'No. Several reasons. One—I want to see you walk out of that door first. Think you can make it in a couple of months?'

'Of course. Do you think I can?' he asked seriously, while some hope appeared in his eyes, lifting the frown.

'When we can get your arm strong enough to manipulate two sticks, or even a frame, you'll be doing just that,' she said encouragingly. 'It's just a question of patience and time.'

'I don't have enough of either.'

'You will find both. . .'

'I've forgotten how it feels to be upright and not at this angle,' he grumbled. 'And as for swinging up on to my horse—I'd give anything for that.'

'It will happen. You're improving faster than we expected.'

'Is that so?' He looked up eagerly.

'Yes. It is. Dr Patterson has to go to London for a seminar next month and he would like you to be manipulative by then.'

'Why,' he asked thoughtfully, 'should he find you an apartment? Are you and he—or shouldn't I ask?'

'You shouldn't ask. But I'll tell you. He's going with me so that I don't have any slip-ups, being the greenhorn that I am about contracts and legalities. Also, I don't have a clue where addresses are—nor how far from the hospital, and I need to be on a bus route and fairly near to the shops. Neither have I a clue how much one pays, or of dollar exchange values.'

'Besides all that, you want him to help you.'

'Yes. I suppose so. He has been so supportive all through.'

'Sure. I'll have the brown top today; and I do have a robe somewhere.'

'Yes. It's here. You want it on now?'

'Oh—sure. Even if I can only get one arm in a sleeve. OK?' He looked up for her inspection when they were finished.

'Fine. Now I'm convinced your visitor is a lady.'

'No. It isn't,' he said regretfully. 'Will you get this letter in the post for me?'

'Yes, I'll do it now.'

When Neil Patterson, his head down and walking fast, passed her, not noticing her, she was surprised when she heard him call her name.

'Oh—er—Nurse Hillier.'

She swung round. He was coming back. He looked pale, as if he had been through a long session.

'I haven't been to see Mike today. How is he?'

'Perturbed by a few personal problems but otherwise he seems to be making good progress, Dr Patterson.'

'Good. I might manage it later on. Had rather a shattering morning in OR. I'm needed again apparently—perhaps afterwards.'

He was gone. She had avoided looking at him too intently, remembering last night's kisses which he had probably quite forgotten anyway. But Sarah was hanging on to any threads of human contact simply because of her own splintered emotions, and because it was the only way she would get through the weeks and months ahead. It could be that Dr Patterson thought that way too—or did he genuinely enjoy being with her, the way it had seemed last night?

The first apartment block he took her to see that evening looked rather ostentatious, its foyer flaring with bright lighting, the cars in the forecourt huge and affluent looking.

'Oh, dear,' Sarah groaned. 'I think this place looks far too grand for me. I'm a working girl.'

'We may as well take a look while we have a key,' Neil said, already getting out of the car and coming to open the door for her. She was busy watching the comings and goings of clients through the swing doors and couldn't imagine it becoming her new home at all.

But they went inside on to thick orange carpeting, hearing the piped music, and were directed through to the back of the building.

Going along a corridor, Neil explained that the penthouses were at the top of the building commanding the best view, but there were always single-bedroom apartments somewhere on the ground floor. 'I've been in here before, actually.'

'Oh,' she murmured, as he stopped at number three A. 'This must be it.'

The windows were small, looking out on to grey walls and a yard. Sarah immediately felt closed in. The bedroom had the usual stereotyped furniture and the kitchen and bathroom were adequate but claustrophobic.

'OK. We'll go and see the others on your list.' He smiled patiently.

The next was also in the downtown area and Sarah liked it immediately.

'There are still three others,' he reminded her, amused by her enthusiasm.

'No. I like this. It's just what I want, so there's no point, is there?'

'If you're sure.' He was looking in the cupboards.

'Yes. I love the kitchen and bathroom—and the bedroom is quiet and cosy. It is important when you have to sleep during the day. One needs to be able to switch off. Sometimes I wonder how I ever coped in London. Noisy, cold corridors and rooms like prison cells. It's not usually like that anywhere now, though. That's why it was nicer at St David's. A rota system and my bedroom at home. Oh. . .' Her mouth trembled; she turned away but his arm pulled her towards him; her head slipped on to his shoulder and his arms were comforting. 'I'm sorry.'

'Don't be. It will go on being like this for a very long time,' he told her seriously. 'You must expect it.'

After a moment she asked, 'Do I need to confirm it tonight? I expect they have an answering service, don't they?'

'Probably. You can pop into the office tomorrow some time, but do confirm it—if this is the one.'

'Yes. It's fine. It will be nice to have my own corner to come back to. I am so grateful for your help, Neil. Wonder when I can take it over?'

'Tomorrow, I imagine, if you like. It's vacant.'

'Tomorrow, then. I'll have to go shopping for some food first.'

'That shouldn't be difficult. Shops stay open half the night here. I'll give you a hand to move in.'

She turned to thank him as they reached the door, her eyes, limpid in the half-light, filled with true gratitude.

He was aware then of her attraction for him, wanting suddenly to make her aware of it too. The urge had to be quickly suppressed. She was not ready for any deep involvement yet. Her emotions were too confused. All she wanted, he knew instinctively, was what he had so far given. A warm trusting friendship away from the hospital. When their relationship did move into a more intimate zone—it would be a very exciting one. He could wait.

'What,' she said, unaware of the depth of his thoughts as they came out into the forecourt, 'would I have done without your help?'

'You would have managed. Are you hungry? Have you eaten?'

She shook her head. 'I'm not really hungry, though.'

'I am.' He backed the car and turned north, giving her a side-smile.

'Where are we going?'

'To Peppi's. Hope you like spaghetti. I think it fits the bill tonight. His is the best in town.'

'Sounds exciting.' She slid down into her seat, relaxing utterly.

It was after ten when they arrived back at the Sutcliffes' house. Sarah had phoned and explained that they were going apartment-hunting, and Neil didn't come in with her.

'I've brought some case notes home with me,' he said when they stopped at the gate. 'You won't mind?'

'Of course not.'

His kiss was singular, though quite potent, and she went inside with a rather odd sensation, as if whole new areas were opening up, and yet there was a feeling of needing to tread carefully. Would Neil be one of her first visitors at the apartment? Was she hoping that he might be? Did he intend to go on singling her out in this way? It had rather a daunting, yet exciting effect as she began to see that the whole thing could develop into some kind of relationship. Was it simply because he felt sorry about what had happened to her? Or because he found her attractive enough to. . .? Here her thoughts came to a sudden stop. There was conversation coming from the lounge. They obviously had visitors, but Andrea came out and invited her in just the same.

'Well—if you don't mind, I'll go up and get my things together,' she explained. 'I've got an apartment and Dr Patterson is helping me move in tomorrow—at least, I hope I can get it finalised by then, so please excuse me.'

'That's great news. Of course, you go and do what you like, honey. But don't think you aren't welcome. It's Dr Geerling—have you met him? From the hospital.'

'No. I've heard of him—but I'll go on up, I think.'

Dr Geerling was the top anaesthetist at the hospital and Sarah was quite sure he wouldn't be a bit put out by not meeting a temporary special nurse whom he might never see.

Next morning, Sarah had officially taken over the apartment on a monthly basis and that same evening Neil drove her back to the Sutcliffes' for her cases and for last goodbyes before making the return trip downtown.

'We'll pick up some food on the way,' he said, 'while I'm here with the car.'

'Oh—I can't let you do all this for me. You must have other things you want to do.'

'Sarah—I want to help in any way I can. I think I feel kind of responsible in some way.'

'Oh—you mustn't.'

His hand gripped hers firmly. He opened his mouth to say something but closed it again: she wondered what. And quite soon he left, after making sure that everything was working properly. She hadn't imagined him being conversant with the 'utilities' as he called them, but he evidently was.

'Goodnight,' he murmured. 'I hope you won't feel

too strange.' He made no attempt to kiss her, just closed the door after him.

Sarah never minded being alone, but real loneliness was defined as not being able to be with someone you loved. And it was true, and quite different, from being by oneself. So occupying herself with getting the food put away and finding places for her own things took up the next couple of hours, and then she was ready for an early night, though sleep was evasive and it was after one o'clock when she at last put down her magazine and turned off the light.

She missed the sounds she had come to know. The clatter of utensils, feet in the corridor, girls chattering, doors banging, an ambulance siren—all of which would be welcoming right now. A few cars came and went from the forecourt and a neon sign blazed on and off across the street, zigzagging yellow and blue stripes on to her bedroom wall.

Her thoughts before she slept went to the rancher. His nights were like hers. He was as much out of his environment as she. And missing his Monique. Because he had to be very much in love with that girl with the vibrant personality and flashing dark eyes. Even Sarah had felt her impact. Maybe it was this clash of wills and temperament which constituted the challenge, keeping their relationship alive. It was a very private thing possibly, and not for her to intrude upon. They must have become used to each other if they had been close from schooldays anyway. But there had been a conflict going on last night when she had left; she had known it. It was as she'd finished making him more comfortable before coming away that he had looked hard at her, his voice bitter.

'Sarah—I'd rather be dead than not be fit enough to keep up with the next man. Monique knows I mean that. She told me once that she likes her men tough and challenging, whatever that means. I can't stand her seeing me like this, or anyone else for that matter. Nor this aimless existence, for that's all it is.'

'You're going to be fine, Mike,' she had assured him with conviction. 'It's patience you're a little short of, not courage.'

So she had left him gazing out at the low, fast-moving clouds covering a watery sun, hiding the red and gold streaks of sun rays behind the mountain.

His first question next morning was, 'So—did you get yourself an apartment?'

'Yes. And not too far from here. It's small, but that's what I needed. I feel very independent now.'

'Good.'

'And have you got all your problems into perspective?'

'I guess so. I called Joe and cleared up a few points.'

'I'm staying on at the hospital, Mike. As part of the staff.' She imparted the news to him because it was still new to herself, having just been to what in England would be the nursing officer's room and signed her contract.

'That's great news.'

'Well—I do have to go to the UK for a few days some time fairly soon, but they appreciate that. By then you'll be on one of the open wards, I expect.'

'By then I'll be back at the ranch, I hope.'

'That's good thinking.' Though quite improbable, she knew.

And later that day, when she met Neil along the corridor as she returned from the dispensary with her list, he was delighted to see her, although his white coat and demeanour naturally put some restraint on the situation.

'How *is* our rancher today?'

'No real problems.'

'Good. I'll see him later. And the apartment?'

'Nice. I need to settle in, of course.'

'I'd like to show you where I live some time. Soon, I hope.'

Tentatively she raised her eyes but a siren blared as an ambulance sped towards the entrance gates and he was off, striding down the corridor lightly, while she bemusedly went on her way too.

Down below in the yard a patient was being unloaded and hurried into casualty. Gradually she was getting into the hospital set-up and now that she was recognised by most of the staff, who knew about the tragedy, she found them all ready to be friendly; even an occasional smile or word in passing made all the difference.

A few days later Sarah received another letter from England. Her solicitors advised her early return, if only for a few days, to go through the house contents. They could then get it on the market since she had decided not to keep it going and everything now belonged to her.

'So,' she told Neil as he dropped her off that evening, 'I must go, although I shall hate it. What a task, sorting through it all; and yet it could be burgled or something and I would feel I should have done it sooner. It is my responsibility now. I suppose I have to face up to it.'

'I agree. So why don't you try to get on the same flight as myself? That will be two weeks on Friday to return the following Monday week.'

'That would be wonderful. I'll phone the airport. What's your flight number?'

'I'll have my secretary do it first thing in the morning. Leave it with me, Sarah.'

He leaned across and opened the door, touching her cheek with one finger, but his eyes were saying so much more.

He came along, making an early visit to Mike next morning, handing her a slip of paper with her flight number and booking confirmation on it.

'Thanks,' she said gratefully.

He smiled conspiratorially and went on into the room but a moment later was called to intensive care with a cardiac failure, so he left at once.

She saw him next an hour later as he was about to leave his room, but called her into it instead and closed the door.

'I'm just coming along to room six, but I thought you might bring me up to date. What do you think about getting Mike on to a four-bed ward next week? General nursing? Shall I suggest it? Because you won't be here, will you? And I don't want any setbacks at this stage.'

'He'll be thrilled about that. Some light at the end of the tunnel.'

'Is he that depressed?'

'I'm afraid so.'

'Personal problems?'

'Partly. His girlfriend seems to be keeping away. He thinks it's because of his injuries. And business worries too, I suspect. He feels at such a disadvantage mainly.'

'I see. I'll come and assess him. It might be a good idea to integrate him with fellow sufferers. He's a nice guy under that aggressive exterior.'

'That's just it. He isn't the aggressive type at all. Arrogant. Very angry and frustrated, of course. Who wouldn't be? But a normally strong-minded, responsible man. I've learned to understand him—up to a point—and I feel terribly sorry for him.'

He gave her a concentrated look before saying, 'OK. We'll see what can be done about getting him out of that one room.'

'Thank you, Dr Patterson,' this for the ears of a staff nurse who had knocked and been admitted and given Sarah an odd glance. And that was the last thing she wanted—to have her name coupled with the surgeon now that she was officially on the hospital staff. In future she must not be seen talking privately to him for his sake as well as her own. But what would they make of the fact that she and he were flying out on the same plane? Perhaps they needn't know.

Mike decided to go into the other ward.

'When I get back,' Sarah said, 'I expect you'll be out of bed for part of each day.'

'I hope your expectations are realised,' he said slowly, looking up at her, aloof in his attitude since he had known she was going with Dr Patterson.

His eyes were very blue now that he was not being sedated so much; almost intense in their perusal of her.

It bothered her. Surely he couldn't think that she and Neil were anything but travelling companions? Yet was it important—what he made of it?

Quietly she finished straightening his bed and just then the door opened and Dr Patterson came in with another surgeon, going straight to the patient, so Sarah had to follow as no sister was around.

'Hi, there, Mike. This is Dr Ralph Fuller, chief of surgery. He would like to have a look at you.'

'Yes. I'm impressed at the rapidity of your post-operative recovery, considering the rather poor state you were in when we first saw you.'

Mike's frown was back. 'Then you must know that I'm more interested in when I can go out rather than the way I came in, Dr Fuller.'

'You're in a hurry, Mr Rayner. I seem to have heard that somewhere before. These guys on orthopod are a clever lot and they aren't going to keep you here a moment longer than necessary.'

He was examining the X-ray plates as he spoke and Sarah, standing quietly behind him holding the case notes file, saw them too.

'Hmm. . .' Dr Fuller began, 'there are a lot of intrinsic happenings under those plasters, aren't there? You couldn't have had a nice clean break, could you?'

Sarah cringed, but as the two doctors conferred, moving towards the door, she saw that Mike had gritted his teeth and shut off too. Just as they closed the door after them the phone rang on her table. 'It's Joe,' she told him, bringing it close by his bed. She left the room then. Just in case he should want to ask about Monique. There had been no news of her since that afternoon as far as she knew, neither had he mentioned her after that one outburst, although she could have phoned any evening when Sarah was not there. Only somehow she didn't think so. Neither did he pass on any of the ranch news when she returned half an hour later.

Debby had been behind her in the queue for the early evening meal and joined Sarah at the table, carefully avoiding direct mention of her tragedy, but commiserating definitely over Mike Rayner.

'I could have slapped him, Sarah—and more than once, when you were away for those two days. He's worse than a child. Gee—more like a bear in a cage.'

'Yes,' Sarah said thoughtfully. 'I think that's a very apt description, and why he is finding it unbearable to be bed-nursed, Debby. I feel so sorry for him.'

'But you mustn't get that involved—I couldn't do anything right. It was, "Nurse Hillier doesn't do it that way," or simply being ordered to go away. Doesn't he get to you?'

'Perhaps it's because I am involved,' Sarah said quietly. 'I feel—I owe him everything I can do to make him not mind so much.'

'Dangerous, that, isn't it?'

'Probably. But he seems to need me around, so we'll take it from there.'

He was certainly thinking a lot today. So what was going on up at the ranch? He obviously didn't intend telling Sarah.

Next morning when Mike touched his unshaven chin speculatively she knew what was coming, and waited with both hands resting on the high bed while she studied the face on which she was about to start working.

CHAPTER SEVEN

MIKE'S eyes seemed a deeper blue today. Now they flashed across Sarah's and focused. 'Am I getting rid of these excruciating bits of wire at last?'

'They're not wire—they're——'

'Am I?'

'Yes. You are. I'll fetch the stitch-cutters.' As he rested his head against his pillows, she said lightly, 'It's bound to hurt a bit, Mike, because it's still very sore and I'll be tweaking a few hairs—but I'll be as careful as I can.'

'Just—get it over,' he ground out between clenched teeth, jerking his head away from her hand on his forehead to steady it.

'You must keep still,' Sarah murmured, her face just above his own while she concentrated. 'These stitches are very small, for obvious reasons.'

One by one they were discarded and he didn't move.

'Your soap smells of sandalwood,' she remarked when she turned back to him.

'Oh?' He appeared disinterested in small talk so she kept silent. It was clear that the whole thing was proving an ordeal for him. But then, as she leaned over him, the scent of her, though faint and elusive, reminded him suddenly of wild honeysuckle which grew in the foothills around his ranch. And a wave of longing—almost like the homesickness one felt at an enforced stay away from home in the growing-up years—engulfed him. And he could hardly bear it. What was he doing down here in the big city, like a moose with its legs caught in a trap? He closed his eyes.

'There's just one suture left, Mike,' she was saying.

'It's a little messy, so I'll leave it another day or two.' Straightening up, she regarded him professionally. 'You should feel a lot more comfortable now.'

'Thanks,' he said briefly. 'At least I can open my mouth.' He swung his good arm up. 'What about these?'

'Those must be left too. They're a bit tougher and deeper,' she told him firmly. 'Just don't go throwing that arm around too much. We're going in the right direction now.'

'My face feels very sore.'

'I know. The stiffness will soon go now. That's quite enough for one day,' she said, seeing that his reading material was to hand before she went off to arrange his meals for that day.

When Neil saw him later on as Sarah was taking his tray away, he raised his eyebrows because it had been barely touched, and went straight to the point.

'I don't want you trying to exist on fruit alone, Mike. You're getting much too lean. Have a shot at getting your system back to normal. You'll soon be needing some back-up energy. Nurse Hillier is trying to do all she can to make it appetising. You're a lucky guy.' He examined his face and hands since the sutures had been removed. 'Mmm—they look a bit angry still, but they're healing well.'

Sarah, watching Mike, now looked across the bed at his surgeon. He was looking at her and as their eyes met the chemistry was back. She was so aware of his magnetism now that her heart seemed to lift, and before she made a pretence of straightening her patient's sheet the colour rose in her face.

Neil had seen her blush and felt an elation of his own. But now was not the time or place. He hadn't seen her away from the hospital at all during the last week for various reasons. One, that he was working on his notes for the coming London conference. Another, that Sarah was now living on her own and, somehow, it wasn't quite the same as when she'd been with the Sutcliffes. He must give her time to settle in and reassess the way her whole life was changing. Besides which, there was always a chance that when she returned to England and her home, ties would be too strong and she just might decide to stay. He steeled himself to wait. He hadn't come this far without acquiring patience and this was especially important now, when this girl had come into his life and everything about her had become so special, so different. He needed to see her every day. He was haunted by her face, her lovely femininity every night. He knew now that she was the only woman in the world he wanted to be with, for the rest of his life. But he couldn't tell her. Not yet.

A week later Mike was transferred, bed and all, to one of the wards through the corridor. There were two other patients also there, one a rodeo rider with a spinal injury, and a logger from up-river who had fallen between the logs being roped together on the banks. He had a smashed upper arm and was hooked up to lateral traction, but he was in a lot of pain, and because of his huge biceps the bone fragments couldn't stay set close enough, so he was scheduled for more surgery and open reduction for next morning.

'You'll be on duty here for the rest of today and tomorrow, Nurse Hillier,' Sister Green, a stand-in sister, explained, 'and, I suppose, until Dr Patterson takes you away for his next private patients.'

As yet Sister Green didn't know of her arranged trip to England. But she soon would have to know.

'So,' Mike said, almost under his breath as she put his things away in his locker, 'it's not all bad, if you're to be around.'

And later, when the logger began his grouse about having more surgery, it was Mike who quietly told him in no uncertain terms that if the surgeon thought it needed doing again, then it did. And there was only one thing to do: take it and shut up.

At which Sarah allowed herself an amused smile behind the door of the medicine cupboard.

That night, everyone and everything was left behind at the hospital when she arrived at her apartment. There were flowers at the porter's desk. From the Sutcliffes.

'To welcome you home,' the card said.

It was thoughtful of them and she felt grateful. But home to her could never be a three-roomed flat. Home meant a latticed-windowed house in England—in a Dorset town where the hills were always in sight. Where she must soon go and systematically work at dismantling all there was of her past. Yet—did she really have to do that? 'Oh—Sarah-Jane,' she said brokenly, 'you're a sucker for punishment, that's for sure.'

Yet before she went to bed her case was already half-full and she had begun to look forward to the long journey with Neil beside her. Perhaps they would get to know each other even better sitting in the close proximity of an airline seat. Because he had been to the flat it was easier to think of him as she lay quietly in bed after turning out the light. It was his eyes, full of expression, that danced between her and the wall.

The next day was a full one—with the logger down for surgery and another patient brought in from an accident outside, his motorcycle a twisted heap of metal on the highway—and a full eight hours of responsibility in a fresh environment meant that Sarah was aching from head to toe by evening.

Each of these men needed a different level of nursing. It was a trauma ward, often as the result of accidents; so unexpectedly were they in hospital that nurses had to be observant and help with investigations on admittance, and Sarah had been absorbed in such real nursing all that day.

She was relieved to find that Mike had decided to settle too. Perhaps his realisation that the other two men were just as anxious as himself about being able to cope afterwards had something to do with it.

But when he was also washed and made comfortable and Sarah had handed him his comb one morning a few days later, he asked coolly, 'What time do you leave on Friday?'

'Mid-afternoon. I see you're keeping your beard.' She eyed him critically.

'I've grown attached to it.'

'Obviously,' she giggled, deliciously he thought, only nothing gave that away.

'I would like to see a little more flesh on your bones when I get back.'

He avoided her eyes, saying grimly, 'I do look rather cavernous, I suppose.'

'Oh, I wouldn't go as far as that. And you *will* do all the right things while I've gone, Mike? I shall wonder how you are——'

'Not for a moment, Nurse Hillier. Your thoughts won't veer in this direction when you're with our eminent Dr Patterson. No way—after all, why would you set up your flight together? There'd be no point. Would there?'

She quickly finished tidying his locker and put his toilet-bag and towel away before pushing her trolley out into the corridor. Neither of them had said another word. Just as well she was going to be away for a time. He was really getting to her. How dared he impose his antagonism on her? It had nothing to do with him that she and Neil were travelling together, yet he obviously resented the fact. She would have to ignore it for the rest of the day. Besides, as it happened, she was too busy to do otherwise and when she at last came off duty she couldn't remember having felt so tired mentally and physically for a long time, kicking off her shoes when she reached her flat and walking barefoot around it for the rest of the evening.

Mike was out of bed next day, his legs still encased in plaster casts, very evident and awkward-looking. Someone had put a bed-table beside him and propped him up. His irritation was growing every minute, but today Sarah was very occupied with the other patients and two first-years were assigned to help with him and the rodeo rider—at least their more material needs, although she kept an eye on him.

He picked at his savoury mince and spaghetti lunch, demanding instead a crisp roll and cheese. 'And maybe some fresh fruit,' he shouted after the nurse who had already had enough of him.

Glancing towards his bed, Sarah saw that his dish was empty. She must try to remember to get him some oranges and grapes later.

Supper that night was again refused. Suddenly she felt too tired to care.

'OK, Mike,' Sarah told him firmly, 'if you don't want to eat. It's your life.'

'It is, isn't it?' he answered coolly.

'Yes. Well—I'm off now. Don't let me down,' she begged.

He didn't reply but watched her crisp white figure, the cap a little tilted towards the back on top of the shining hair, until she had disappeared completely. Then he shut off and didn't attempt to socialise with the other patients, and they were too low themselves to care.

For Sarah everything had a new look now. From the moment she left her apartment to drive with Neil to the airport, the hospital receded into yesterday. At the booking desk there was a choice of seats and they could sit together for the long flight to Heathrow, London, where they hoped to arrive at seven the following morning, British time.

It was a lovely June day, the first really hot one of

the summer, so Sarah travelled in a cool green dress and sandals, with her soft woollen coat at the ready, knowing the English summer. Neil had taken off his jacket, and looked cool and relaxed in his fine cotton shirt as they made their way to the departure lounge to wait.

Once airborne they became engrossed in their various reading material, his mainly to do with his conference, she being determined not to encroach in any way if he wanted to be quiet. There was enough chatter going on all around anyway, and the snacks and drinks were already underway.

She slept a little, although he didn't. When awake they talked desultorily but not about anything in particular and, although she felt a little shy at first because he seemed different—out of context and a little out of reach—she soon settled down to their new, rather cramped environment. Besides, she could watch him without his being aware of it.

Far below the ice-floes could be clearly seen and above the sky was still bright blue and blazing sunshine for a time.

When dinner was served they talked easily, as if they had always been travelling companions, and even the silences didn't matter as the plane took them across the vast expanses of icebergs and sea, and everything seemed just a little unreal, as though they had both taken off into another era.

When she yawned, he grinned, shaking his head at her apology. 'We would be asleep if we were back there—strange: one never catches up on those lost hours.'

They both dozed after that; the talking had ceased all through the plane, except for one or two of the children, restless and not able to settle. It seemed in no time at all that the passengers were being woken up and blankets collected and the smell of coffee wafted

across, a welcome sign that it was breakfast-time. Neil
went off to freshen up, and Sarah did too.

They were going to arrive in good time, now crossing
the Scottish coast far below, tiny islands and the green
of the foothills, then below them were sandy beaches
and moors, towns and cities, and at last the metropolis;
they flew low over the Thames, hovering until they
went in to land, and then came the grinding of tyres on
the runway.

'We're here,' Neil said, stretching his stiff limbs.
'OK, Sarah?'

'Fine,' she answered, standing up and slinging her
cream straw bag over her shoulder while she picked up
her flight-bag and coat and followed him along the
aisle.

Standing outside the terminal while they waited for
their taxi to come up, Sarah knew that she was home.
Her territory. It inspired confidence. At her instigation
they shared the cab into London; also the cost of the
fare.

'I'd like to go straight to Waterloo,' she told him
when he asked if she would like breakfast at his hotel.

'Can I phone you? At your home? I've got the
number here somewhere. You will be OK?'

They were already deafened by the noise of the
trains and traffic.

'Of course I will. It has to be done. I'm among
friends. So we'll meet at the airport terminal, then, on
the eighteenth. One-thirty flight. And—do call me
some time, won't you?' she asked wistfully.

'Sure. I'll be here. Have a good week, Sarah. Don't
let it get to you too much.' He gripped her hands. 'I'll
be thinking of you. . .' He kissed her lightly.

'Thank you. I'll remember that.'

Waterloo station in the morning rush-hour had to be
the busiest in the country, she decided as she made her
way to the indicator to check out her train. The ticket-
queue was already forming and so she picked up her
case, slung her bag over one shoulder and joined it.

I'm home—home, she thought as she looked round.
Somehow people seemed different. She didn't know
what the difference was. Was it apathy? Certainly
different, less colourful, and no one seemed to smile or
even appear interested. Vancouver was now very far
away, and so was Mike.

The queue was moving forward and, once through
the barrier and comfortably settled in her seat, she
gave herself up to enjoy the sun-drenched fields, cattle
under the spreading oaks, hamlets, thatched cottages
and back gardens which reached down to the line as
the train hurtled through non-stop until it reached
Southampton.

Next stop Bournemouth, and here she changed to
the slower train which at last drew into the sleepy little
station where most passengers alighted for the sandy
beaches of the Dorset coast.

Was it only three hours since she had said goodbye
to Neil? She could imagine him already meeting up
with medical colleagues and the interest and stimu-
lation of medics sharing views and observances in their
own field of medicine.

The taxi taking her to the house went through the
high street and past the wistaria-covered offices of her
lawyers, the blue flowers growing like bunches of
grapes over the Georgian building. Just as she had
remembered them. She wished she could show Neil
this part of the world. It was as the car turned into the
avenue leading away from the county town towards the
brick houses on the outskirts that her heart felt heavy
in her body and she sat upright in the taxi.

'Number seven,' she told the driver, and when he
stopped she could hardly believe it was the same house.
It looked neglected, as if someone had left it in a hurry,
which indeed she had. The grass was quite high, and
the tiled doorstep dirty and unpolished.

She put her key in the door and stepped over an

avalanche of envelopes and newspapers and magazines which hadn't at first been cancelled.

Everything looked different as she went from room to room, the sadness when she saw her father's things almost strangling her. Her throat ached. 'No. . .' she said aloud, 'I don't want to stay here. I'm going back.'

She made coffee and drank it hot and strong. Then she telephoned Mr Attwood. There was, it seemed, so much to be done. He had a prospective buyer for the house, if she still wished to sell.

'But don't, please, Sarah, make any fast decisions.'

'I am going back to Vancouver, Mr Attwood. I haven't yet finished what I need to see through there. When can we meet?'

'Can you come into my office in the morning? Say— eleven o'clock. We'll go through it all.'

'Yes—goodbye.'

Sarah looked wearily round the hall and through the open doors of the rooms, unaware of the tears on her cheeks. Then she picked up her bags and took them up to her bedroom. Just where did one start? A whole houseful of furniture? Should she let it furnished? It was a thought, but she knew immediately that it was not the answer. There was an emptiness here that could never be different. She was going to have to make a new start, a home of her own, somewhere else, leaving her memories behind.

Jet lag—that's what's wrong with me, she decided; I need lots and lots of sleep. But that would have to wait. Right now she was going to change into old jeans and a cotton top and get started.

She began by opening all the windows. This brought Mrs Beales to the back door, and everything came tumbling back as they sat in the kitchen and Sarah brought her up to date with all that had happened in Canada.

No one, Sarah decided when she had gone, was going to completely understand why she had come home simply to clear out the house, sell it, and go back to Vancouver again. Not even when she explained about Mike Rayner. Surely there were other nurses who could help him recover? Why her?

Why indeed. It had been her own decision and fortunately she had been able to make that choice.

At the end of the day she felt exhausted and knew she must stop and get some food. Mrs Beales had brought her eggs and a few necessities like bread, milk, coffee and tea, and tomorrow was another day.

At nine o'clock she decided to have a hot bath and an early night. She was almost out on her feet. She was halfway up the stairs when the phone rang. The same phone, the same time as before. The same voice, only this time her fears were dispersed. She had never been so glad to hear Neil.

'Hi, there—Sarah?'

'Oh—it's so good to hear you. I was just going to have a bath.'

'How interesting,' he said teasingly. 'Are you alone?'

'Of course I'm alone.'

'How are things? How are you?'

'Oh—it's difficult to put into words.'

'You haven't changed your mind. You don't want to stay?'

'Oh, no. It—nothing's the same. I can't just pick up the pieces. I'm glad I've made the decision to stay in Canada—at least for the time being. Mr Attwood is going through it all with me tomorrow and after that it just means sorting out what can go into storage and what will have to be sold. It's very difficult to explain, but other than a few special things and my own, of course, I don't want to see any of it again.'

'Those are healthy decisions, Sarah.'

She said, 'Now—tell me about you. How is your hotel?'

'Fine. I'm very comfortable. I've already met a nice lot of guys. It looks like being a good week. Like you,

I'm a bit jet lagged, and will soon turn in. Just wanted to make sure you're OK.'

'I'm fine, especially now. Goodnight, Neil.'

'Night, Sarah.'

'Thank you. . .' she whispered, as she replaced the receiver. He knew exactly how she would be feeling, and had taken the trouble to do something about it.

Next morning she was in the lawyer's office at the appointed time, his old-world courtesy as he seated her in an armchair and offered again his commiserations just as she'd remembered.

Mr Attwood became a dignified rock to whom she clung like a limpet when things became too complicated.

The next day, on impulse, Sarah called Sister Maine towards evening at her flat and found her there.

'It's my day off tomorrow, Sarah. Do let me come and give a hand. We have so much news to catch up on. You don't *have* to go back, though, do you?'

'Yes—I'm afraid so. But come tomorrow, please.'

Sister tried to persuade her not to stay in Canada for too long, although she had now been replaced at St David's. Sarah told her about Mike Rayner. After that she made no further appeal, listening while they drank coffee together in the kitchen, surrounded by china and tea boxes for packing because Sarah had decided to keep some of the things and have them stored. Some time she might want to furnish a flat of her own.

'Your rancher is going to count the days until you get back,' Sister observed.

'Mmm. Yes, I think he might. His recovery is far too slow for his peace of mind.'

'What were his injuries?'

Sarah gave her the details. 'And his left leg was a fractured tibia and fibula. The other, fragmented fractures—quite a bit of splintering, Dr Patterson said. He operated.'

'Poor man. Both legs. And the arm?'

'Smashed and fragmented too. He was hooked up on lateral traction for the first few days, so was literally helpless. So there were facial lacerations—oh, he looked a mess. Shock too, of course. We've had it all before, I know. But I felt specially sorry for him. He resisted so hard—and the accident should never have happened, so. . .'

'You feel responsible? For your father?'

'Yes. I suppose so. In a way.'

She spoke about the Sutcliffes and all the help and comfort she had received from them, and about Dr Patterson, and Sister saw the quick flush on her cheeks and a faraway look in the green eyes.

'He flew over with me. Now he's at a conference in London for the week, but we'll be going back on the same flight. He's been marvellous. He helped me with finding an apartment, even moving me in.'

'Married?'

'Oh, no. Very much a bachelor, by choice I should think. His work comes first in his life and everything else a well-ordered second.'

'So,' Sister remarked conclusively as she got back to wrapping china in tissue paper, 'one thing seems certain—I'm not likely to drag you away from your new interests and back to St David's.'

'I—don't think I could settle there again, Sister,' Sarah told her with trembling mouth. 'It's better this way. A new beginning.'

'You *will* keep in touch, won't you?'

'Of course. I could never forget you,' Sarah said simply.

Neil called her twice more during the week, and on Monday they would be flying back together.

At last the house stood empty. The furniture had gone to the salerooms and Sarah's own possessions into storage for the future. All the painful tasks were accomplished. Goodbyes said. Friends promised that if and when she came home again she would be in touch.

A part of her life was now behind her forever; except in her mind and the last tears.

When Sarah entered the terminal, having come part of the way by train then across country by coach from Woking so that she hadn't even touched London, Neil had already booked in. He stood at the top of the escalator, looking down on her for a few moments while she waited for her boarding pass and got her luggage weighed in. More than she had come over with, he noticed.

As she turned her head, her hair, shining and soft, seemed to bounce with new lustre. She looked competent, changed in some way. But she always had something he admired in a woman, a way of wearing her clothes, carefully chosen and then forgotten, and her head high.

Today was one of those cool June days, part of the English summer. He was delighted to see her as he went two steps at a time down the moving staircase to join her. And it showed. Her blush deepened as he caught up with her.

So how could she not feel elated when his arm slipped through hers and he murmured, 'Hi,' against her ear? Any girl would feel flattered. He was that kind of man, with an intelligent face, yet often thoughtful; one would never be quite sure of his intentions, though, which increased the excitement. If that was what one wanted in a man. She walked happily by his side—happy because she would be sitting next to him for the next nine hours at least.

Over pre-flight drinks in the departure lounge they exchanged comments on their week's activities.

Last evening for Neil had been the dinner and social culmination before breaking up. Like Dr Sutcliffe he had a lot of reading matter to go through and felt stimulated by new techniques, lectures, fresh discoveries, research projects, drug research—and, above all, simply talking 'shop' non-stop for a lot of hours.

'And you, Sarah? Did you accomplish all you had to do?'

'Yes.' She told him of her decision to put some things into storage for when she came back again.

'So you have decided to come back to the UK?'

'Some time, I expect. Who knows?'

Their flight was called then so he had no need to comment further, but he looked thoughtful as they walked to the departure gate. After that it was all routine—finding their seats, strapping up for take-off. England was behind now, and far below them a ship, very small, gleamed on the sunlit waters of the Atlantic.

'We have a long journey ahead, Sarah,' Neil said. 'Mind if I read through some of these?'

'Of course not.' She had too many mixed feelings to want to talk anyway and he had bought magazines for her to read. Besides, she needed to think.

Neil said later, when he had stopped reading to give his order to the steward and hers too, 'Work tomorrow—for both of us. I wonder what has been happening while we've been away.'

She didn't comment at first. An exciting thrust of pleasure ran along her nerves. She would see him each day from now on. 'I like my work,' she said honestly. 'I'll be glad to get back to it, I think.'

'It's nice to have you to travel with,' he said, reaching for his drink and asking for more ice before he suggested, 'I think we should have a night out together soon. I can foresee a hectic few days ahead but it should soon settle down. I thought you just might be tempted to stay in England, Sarah.' He eyed her speculatively over his wine glass.

'No,' she told him coolly. 'I knew I was committed

to return to Vancouver—at least for the rest of the summer. After that—who knows?'

And now, back in Canada once again, travelling towards the city, it was quite different sitting beside Neil from that first time. He dropped her off at her apartment, both jet lagged; it was very late evening by Canadian time, and that night Sarah slept from sheer exhaustion.

Awoken by her alarm-clock next morning, she leapt out of bed to the kitchen, standing in her bare feet while she downed her orange juice, wondering how long it would take her to reach the hospital by bus. She mustn't be late today.

She guessed that Mike would be watching the door for her to appear.

And he was. Although he attempted to disguise the fact, greeting her in an offhand manner when she went straight to his bed, regardless of whether anyone thought it unusual.

'Hello, Mike.' If he heard the concern in her voice, he gave no sign. His mouth was set in a very determined line, his head back on the pillow, while he eyed her discriminatingly.

'So you're back, Nurse Hillier.'

'Yes. I'm back. How have you been?'

'What does it matter? I'm still here, aren't I? How was it over there?'

'Oh—it's still dear little England,' she told him reminiscently. 'Just as green—just as personal. Now tell me—how are you?'

When he didn't reply she reached for his chart. He watched her but looked away the moment she put it back. He was out of traction now but still in plaster.

She didn't think he looked good at all, a little shocked by his pallor beneath the weather-tanned skin although the discoloration had faded now. But his face looked almost haggard and his beard had grown, though someone had trimmed it neatly, as well as his hair. He looked—different.

As she counted out his medication, which had been changed, he asked grudgingly, 'Well—did Dr Patterson come back with you?'

'Yes. He did. I expect he'll be around to see everybody some time today. I'll come back and get you out on to the day-bed in a while, Mike.'

She left him then, picking up where she had left off, checking notes and charts to familiarise herself with any new routine, checking all the way. It was going to be that kind of day, she thought, still feeling the effects of the long flight in spite of a night's sleep.

Later she returned with a male nurse, peeling off Mike's sheet and the cage over his legs.

'Now, put your arm around my neck—so—and just go with us,' she told Mike, sliding her arm under him to meet that of the other nurse and depositing him on the other bed-chair with as little discomfort as possible.

He refused to look at her, ignoring their repartee. How could he know that she was so sorry for him, recognising that weakness was hell for a strong man? So he turned off—pretending to read—while they continued with the other beds in the ward.

Here the men treated nurses as an outlet for any teasing—until they saw by Sarah's manner that they had gone a little too far. This she was used to and knew how to cope with. Besides, there was so much to do that she had no time to talk much. Not a bit like being on a private ward at all.

When she did snatch a few minutes for a coffee-break she heard that 'the rancher guy' had reverted to his withdrawn manner, unless he compared everything they did with Nurse Hillier's way; and twice had asked to be discharged. He was only discouraged by another surgeon's flatly informing him that if he did go now he might never walk again, let alone ride a horse in a round-up.

'Oh, no. How awful,' Sarah groaned. 'What did he say to that?'

'He shut off. Well, he did ask for it. Heavens—we're doing our best. We didn't cause his accident.'

'Neither did he,' she said, having to turn away while she fought back the tears. No matter what she had to do, she was getting that man back on to his feet. If only it hadn't got to be such a long and frustrating business. But bones took time to knit together, tissues time to heal, and nerve-ends to find a home in which to settle, and it was all a very painful process. And, for a man of Mike's calibre, unbearably hard.

CHAPTER EIGHT

THE moment Dr Patterson appeared by Mike's bedside on his rounds later that morning, with two interns and Sister and Sarah among the back-up, he was pressed for a time limit as to how much longer he had to stay here.

'You mean—when can you go?'

'Of course that's what I mean. Next week? If all I'm to do is lie around I can quite easily do that at the ranch.'

'It isn't that simple, Mike. Let's give it another week, then review the situation. I'd like the plasters off and see the X-rays before I can give any decision. Physio can be given at the hospital then—but we haven't reached that stage yet.'

'I've got to be able to see the end of this.'

'I am sorry. It can't be hurried.'

'OK. Another week, then.'

Sarah closed her eyes with relief. She knew that part of his need to get home was Monique. She couldn't ask, of course, and he seemingly didn't want to talk about it. Perhaps he regretted having done so before. But it was more than that. Something was different. He had definitely switched off her since she had gone to England with Neil. Could it be that? If so, why?

At the end of that week Neil took Sarah for an early supper and then on to the Queen Elizabeth Theatre where he had seats for an orchestral concert. She, like Neil, was lost in the music, the surroundings, the belonging feeling, with Neil sitting close to her and enjoying it just as much, by the rapt expression on his face as she gave him a quick glance.

When they came out, he drove her to her apartment

112

as they discussed the music, finding a mutual bond, surprising each other by their basic knowledge of the composer's other works.

'I relaxed entirely,' Neil said. 'Amazing, isn't it, what music can do to help one unwind?'

'I loved every minute,' she said reminiscently. 'Like you—I was completely carried away.'

When he stopped on the forecourt of the apartment block and put his hand over hers in her lap, she asked, 'Would you like to come in for coffee?'

'Perhaps just a quick one. I've got some case notes I want to go through.'

She didn't try to keep him, producing hot coffee promptly, but as they drank it, he looking quite at home in an armchair, one leg poised across his knee, an almost unbearable spear of pleasure shot through her body, an emotion which she could no longer deny. She had to lower her eyes to her coffee-mug so that he couldn't see their expression.

'Can we go out again on Sunday evening?' he suggested after a short silence.

'Twice in one week?' she murmured.

'I enjoy showing you around. Very much. But that will be in contrast to this evening. I'm going to take you to the Greek village.'

'That sounds fascinating.'

'It's fun—especially when there's a ship in, if you don't mind the high spirits of the sailors. It will be an experience and we needn't stay too long.'

'I shall love it. Thank you.'

'Must go now.' He stood up quickly and she followed him into the tiny hall, her eyes raised to his revealingly, so that he lifted her chin and bent his head slowly, his lips finding hers and moving gently over them. His arms were around her, enfolding her, so that she felt deliciously cocooned in them, and her arms slipped behind his shoulders of their own volition, until he raised his head, gazing down at her, and her arms dropped to her sides.

He said firmly, 'Goodnight, Sarah,' and left her.

She stood for a moment, looking at the closed door, feeling slightly bemused, before touching her hot cheeks. Neil's had been just as flushed as her own. Which thought sent her to bed, still with a glow of happiness she refused to relinquish. That kind of feeling just had to be for real. Oh—what a marvellous evening it had been! And now there was Sunday to look forward to as well.

Because of the pressure on the wards she did even more so as the week progressed. But Sarah was used to that, and all three of the orthopaedic patients in the ward needed the same kind of nursing care; some had to have dressings removed and replaced with fresh ones, there was checking for any clot formation or skin problems, and any pain was registered at once and reported.

Sarah was alternating between wards now and not able to see so much of Mike as he obviously wanted. The rest of the staff already had the wrong impression of him, which Sarah did her best to deny.

Sunday came at last.

'We're going to enjoy this evening,' Neil told her as they went through into the restaurant and the music hit them. The atmosphere was terrific and she was caught up in his mood, which was different, a little more abandoned, showing a new side, and certainly one she had never even suspected him of having.

'I haven't always been a surgeon, you know,' he grinned delightedly, when they returned to their table. 'I've had my student days too. I hope you're enjoying it all,' he asked her seriously now.

'Can't you see that I am? It's really fun. I love the Greek costumes, even the noise.'

'It's escapism, isn't it? And you look rather special tonight—I'm a lucky guy.'

'Do you mean that?' she said, half laughing, then had to look away from his ardent expression.

'Do I ever say what I don't mean, Sarah? I—hate subterfuge and don't forgive it in others. You should know that by now, surely.' She didn't reply, overwhelmed by her own feelings and wishing she did know.

He held her more firmly when she slipped into his arms for another dance and this time she couldn't not be aware that his feelings were more passionate towards her, and because he didn't speak, neither did she, returning to their table by mutual consent when the music quickened its tempo. Soon afterwards they left, his mood still with him, and in the car his arm pulled her to him while his mouth searched for hers hungrily, passionately, and her own lips parted under their pressure and she was lost in the swimming of her senses.

'Oh. . .' she gasped breathlessly when he had let her go.

'I think,' he said huskily as he turned the key and switched on, 'that I had better take you home. Unless you would like to come back with me. . .? Coffee? Another drink? Or. . .'

She didn't look away from the ardent, quizzing, almost impatient look directed at her now. 'No—I'd like to go back to my apartment. It's been a long day and tomorrow could be even worse—for you too.'

She was still trembling and he knew it. But he was adept at switching off, and now his voice held a resigned note. 'OK. I don't usually give myself a late night before my day in theatre. There are a few teasers for tomorrow, too. So you made the right decision, Sarah. For us both. I did rather get carried away, and who the hell can blame me?'

He kissed her quickly. There was nothing prolonged about their parting outside on the forecourt of her block either. And strangely she was quite relieved about that because, while she was becoming more sure of her own feelings, she wondered uneasily about his.

But her room gave her new confidence. She enjoyed her independence and needed to be alone sometimes. Time would heal the void left by the loss of her father, though it would have to take years and maybe a lifetime, but there was therapy in her work, so the harder and more time-consuming it was, the better.

The next morning she saw that Mike was watching the door for her. While Sarah opened the windows, letting in the sweet smell of summer blossom from the honeysuckle on the wall, he lay watching her, and he was anything but good-tempered.

'Good morning, Mike. Anything wrong?' she asked as she picked up his chart and took down his thermometer for the first of today's check-ups.

When he didn't answer her at once she knew that something was wrong, so she raised her eyes to his enquiringly—which was what he was waiting for to press home his grievance—if that was what it was.

His first question put her on course.

'Is my room still vacant?'

'I think so. Why?'

'I want it back. Today.'

'Oh. . .but you're getting the same treatment here at far less expense.'

'I don't think finance was mentioned, was it? I'd like it back. Perhaps you'll tell Dr Patterson as soon as possible and arrange it.'

'I will. But he's operating this morning. Unless I catch him before he gets scrubbed up. In any case, you should have consulted Sister-in-charge, not me,' she told him as her cool fingers touched his wrist. 'Oh, Mike, calm down—your pulse is taking off. . .'

'I didn't consult Sister,' he said grimly, 'because she is one of the hazards—as far as I am concerned; and for another, I hate all this backchat. I also prefer—my own nurse around, since it still seems necessary. Don't underestimate me, Sarah. For two shakes I'd discharge myself right now and take the risks.'

'Then you would be very sorry,' she said firmly. Their eyes stayed locked until each was sure the other got the message. Also, Sister had come into the ward and was monitoring the beds one after the other, so he gave in to the necessary ministrations which he couldn't avoid. Sarah was worried about him because once he had made up his mind he would be as good as his word. She knew she would be breaking all the rules. This was something which would never have happened at St David's, but she dared not tell Sister Green. She couldn't bear it if Sister went over to his bed in her rather condescending manner and looked down at him like a bird of prey. In front of the other patients too she would say something like, 'Now, what's all this fuss about, Mr Rayner? Aren't you satisfied with the attention you're getting in here?'

No—she couldn't subject him to that. So, after depositing the soiled dressings in the sluice, she went along to make certain that room six was still unoccupied. Fortunately she caught a glimpse of Dr Patterson about to push open the swing doors of intensive care. She called him quietly. 'Can you spare a moment, Dr Patterson?'

'What is it, Nurse Hillier?'

She finished explaining. 'I thought I should mention it to you first—even Sister doesn't know.'

'Which of course she should, at once.'

'I know. He is rather desperate.'

He glanced at the wall-clock. 'I'll look in after my round here. I think I have time before I scrub up. Suppose he wants you as well.'

'Will I be allowed another move?'

'Do you want to move?'

'If I must.'

'OK. Leave it with me, Sarah. I don't want him to leave here for at least two more weeks—even longer.'

When she told Mike that she had spoken to Dr Patterson his eyes brightened, 'And?'

'He'll be in to see you. But keep it quiet, for heaven's sake.'

'Nurse Hillier—why hasn't this patient had his dressing changed?' Sister's voice rang out from the other side of the room.

Sarah went over to her. 'You said you wanted Doctor to see it first, Sister.'

'Well, do it now, Nurse. . .'

As Sarah went to the cupboard for fresh sterile dressings, Sister Green stumped across to Mike's bed. He lay, his plastered legs uncovered because of the warmth of the sun, his jacket open to his waist, looking at his paper, but not reading.

'Sunning yourself, I see, Mr Rayner. Perhaps it will make you a little less disgruntled.'

'I am not in the least disgruntled, Sister Green,' he said firmly. 'Quite the reverse, in fact.'

'I'm glad to hear it. We should count our blessings. Always somebody worse. You are moving those fingers, I hope—we want you using that arm soon too.'

'Not more than I want it,' he murmured as she departed. Sarah heard him and looked up from her bandaging to send him a conspiratorial smile, without feeling the least bit disloyal to Sister Green, the only one here at the hospital she found it difficult to work with.

That afternoon Mike was wheeled back into the room he had recently vacated. He looked better already.

'But you can't have me all to yourself, Mike,' Sarah said as she went around putting his things away. 'In fact it's a bit of a wangle. One of Dr Sutcliffe's patients has undergone surgery this morning and another lady is in the third room. So instead of another nurse being detailed for these patients, I'm going to look after all three of you.'

'I don't know why I had to be moved out in the first place,' he said, letting out a sigh of sheer relief from his bed halfway out on to the balcony.

It had been because Sarah had been away and a complete stranger would have had to be called in for him, and there were no recruits from the general staff. And it had been thought that being with others would make him more outgoing. It hadn't worked, but she couldn't tell him that.

His next words shattered any complacence. 'I'll only be here for another week or so anyway. Then I shall lay on an ambulance and get myself back to the ranch.'

'Mike—you're not even mobile yet.'

'I'm aware of that. Is it necessary to remind me? Don't you think that if I could get off this bed I wouldn't? I've had enough. I'm accustomed to making my own decisions. I'm going—and you're coming with me.'

'I can't do that——'

'Why not? You're my nurse, aren't you? I'm giving myself a deadline.'

His stormy eyes met hers, blue and steely.

'You are serious?' She never quite knew. But his expression certainly was.

'Of course. I can't expect Midge to take over. She isn't trained and I'll need expert medical supervision, I guess, so I'm inviting you to come up to the ranch. Is there any reason why not? Unless you perfer to be here?'

She avoided the sheer insistence in his compelling gaze, refusing to be intimidated like that. But her heart skipped a beat before she said quietly, 'It will rest with Dr Patterson. Right at this moment you're still hospitalised, so we'll take first things first. Is there anything you need?'

'For God's sake! You sound just like Sister Green,' he muttered irritably.

'So—you're OK. I have to go and see my other patients now, Mike. I'll be back later.'

He nodded, still frowning. 'Thanks.' She knew he was grateful that she had intervened and got him moved back to room six, but it was a grave breach of rules and he was the only man she would have done it for. That in itself was serious.

It wasn't until that same evening, when she and Debby were leaving together, that she heard that Neil had been specially commended.

'It's all round the hospital,' Debby said.

'What is?'

'Dr Patterson. It was the vertebral fusion. Even Mr Holgar wouldn't touch it—must have been very nasty—and he's the neuro-surgeon.'

'Well, she was Dr Patterson's patient originally.'

'Yes. And his decision. He thought the risk involved was fully justified. I suppose she will be one of yours, won't she?'

'I hope so,' Sarah said, proud for Neil's success. He must have known there was always a chance of a chemical irritation to the nerve-roots in this kind of surgery, but he had told her of his own technique. The bone grafting had, in this case, been successful too. He had removed the bits pressing on the nerves and cleared it all out.

'Ginny, up in theatre, told me he was so painstaking over the splinters—they thought they would never get around to cleaning up. Went on for hours.'

'Good for him. Must have been messy. I think's he's a wonderful doctor.'

'And he obviously thinks you're a great nurse,' Debby echoed. 'That's why she's been put on your ward. You and he are quite close—aren't you?'

Sarah could feel the colour rush to her face. 'I don't think. . .'

'I just wondered, having seen you together a couple

of times. Not that I wouldn't give my eye-teeth to change places.'

'It isn't like that, Debby. Don't jump to conclusions.'

It was with some relief that she handed over her duties that evening to the incoming nurses, escaping from the building into the still-warm sun of early evening.

Leaving the hospital atmosphere behind was like shedding a skin; Sarah felt renewed and ready for something stimulating.

She had just showered and slipped into a cotton housecoat when the phone rang.

Neil's voice said, very casually, 'Are you doing anything special, Sarah? If not, would you like to see around Stanley Park? It's too nice to stay indoors.'

'Yes. I would,' she said enthusiastically.

'Right. Pick you up in fifteen minutes. OK?'

When he rang the bell she was waiting, wearing a cotton dress and beige sandals. A cardigan over her shoulders seemed right for this lovely evening. He wore beige close-fitting trousers and a summer shirt; tonight a suede jacket lay on the back-seat of his car.

'You look nice,' he said, sliding into his bucket seat.

'So do you.'

He grinned. 'We do tend to get rather a fixed image at the hospital. Everyone looks so different in ordinary gear. We've been invited to drop in at the Sutcliffes for drinks later.'

'If you won't be too tired? You must have had a gruelling day.'

'Yes. I guess you could call it that. So, do you want to go back to Dr Sutcliffe's?'

'It's a lovely idea.'

He threw her a playful glance. 'Shall we wait and see what evolves before deciding?'

To which she only raised her eyebrows, wondering just what he meant by that.

When dusk fell and the park was floodlit they must

have walked at least halfway around the lake; seen the totem poles which Sarah found awe-inspiring; wandered under the great Douglas firs and she exclaimed at their height, the flower-beds scenting the night air, which brought nostalgia for England and her father's *Nicotiana* beds along the wall on summer evenings.

'And night-scented stocks,' she mused. 'I can almost smell them.' And to Neil's question, 'No—sorry—I'm reminiscing.'

'That is not very complimentary to me, Sarah. I must be slipping. Shall we find the car?'

She stretched her aching toes as he once more slipped into his low seat beside her. 'Now, the Sutcliffes'—or my place?'

'Oh. . .' she decided quickly '. . .the Sutcliffes', I think, since we've been invited—or is it too late?' She met his eyes innocently.

'No. They'll be out on the terrace, being eaten slowly by mosquitos, I expect. I must admit there's a super view over the harbour from their garden.'

'I know. Isn't it strange how quickly we all became socially integrated? Everyone has been awfully nice here.'

'You're that kind of girl. I guess you simply bring out the best in people. Me especially. Haven't you noticed?'

'You're laughing at me.'

'No. I mean it.' He threw her a teasing smile as they turned into the crescent where the Sutcliffes lived. 'Take tonight—you're very delectable, and I'm trying to control my urges to make love to you very thoroughly. It isn't easy.'

'Now I know you are teasing.'

'Want me to prove that I'm not?'

'No,' she said hastily, 'especially not here in their driveway.' She was a little thrown by his words, but already knew he wouldn't have carried out his threat.

But Neil shut off the engine and reached to take her

face in his hands. Before she could move, his mouth
had found hers, forcing her lips apart. While she was
still gasping from the impact he opened the car door
and was looking up at the stars. She had been right.

Skirting the house, Sarah walked beside him over
the lawns to where their hosts, together with two
friends, were sitting in lounge-chairs, talking.

They were both genuinely pleased to see her again
and, while Andrea went for some snacks, Dr Sutcliffe
detached himself from the others to sit beside her,
asking how she was and about her flat and her future
plans after her trip to England.

She was able to talk about those things now, still
very grateful for the way they had helped her through
the trauma of those awful days.

'How is Mike Rayner progressing?'

'Quite well now. But I'm involved with other patients
as well.'

Because she hadn't told Neil of Mike's intentions,
she could not tell Dr Sutcliffe either. But it was really
nice to see him again, away from the hospital, and in
the kitchen she and Andrea also had an exchange of
conversation but from a slightly more womanly angle.

'Do keep in touch. I mean it,' Andrea whispered as
they rejoined the others. And Sarah felt that she really
did. She was so fortunate in her new-found friends.

It was after eleven when Neil dropped her off in the
forecourt. He had kissed her lightly, saying that it was
late, but then, unable to let her go, had kissed her
again, hard, compellingly, one arm around her
shoulders holding her firmly against him.

It was she who drew away and opened the car door,
her face flushed and with burning lips as she stepped
out on the asphalt, glimmering in the sudden shower of
rain.

'Goodnight. . .' she said softly over her shoulder,
not even sure that he would hear her. He watched her

open the swing doors then swung his car out on to the highway.

Sarah decided as she let herself into her apartment that tonight something had changed. She needed time to get her emotive feelings into a proper perspective before she could trust herself with Neil again. Did she want just an affair? Did he?

Neil was also thinking seriously along the same lines. He was normally a disciplined man, but his ardour had been getting out of hand and he had to do something about that. Maybe he shouldn't see Sarah quite so much. But she really was extremely lovely when she was roused. He even began to ask himself just how serious his intentions were regarding her. Because, until now, he had never let any of his private life get out of hand. Nor even let his guard drop nearly as much as it had with Sarah.

But next morning Mike was the man on Sarah's mind. He seemed morose and had something to ask. Was it Monique again? she wondered as she came back to the bed. Had she phoned last night?

'What is it?' she said, looking down at him.

'Has Dr Patterson said when the casts are coming off, Sarah? When I can get out of here?'

'No. Oh, Mike—we had all this out yesterday.'

'I'm simply asking when.' She stood quietly by, studying his face, the strong lines of it; the wide-apart blue eyes very steady, almost piercing today. 'There's a hospital at Hope. They can take over, once my legs are no longer encased in this stuff. Physio—that kind of thing. I mean it, Sarah.'

'I know you do. And you will be transferred soon, but you're not ready yet.'

'Ask Dr Patterson to see me today, please. Do it now.'

Her heart was heavy as she phoned through to his secretary.

Neil came at eleven, just as she emerged from room four with her arms full of sheets.

'What is all this?' he asked briefly.

'I think it's the crunch.'

'Oh—is it? The man's a menace to keep badgering this way.' He pushed open Mike's door.

Oh, dear, Sarah thought as she followed. Neil was not in a good mood at all. Poor Mike.

'Are we back to the same subject?' the surgeon asked him sternly.

Finally, 'Yes, we are. I'm setting my own departure time, Dr Patterson. I'm leaving here next week. Now—plastered legs or no—that's when I'm going. Bear with me. I must get myself back up there. And now—you say your piece. Give it to me straight. You must hate my guts, after all you've done.'

Neil drew a deep breath before answering. But all the time his eyes were assessing Mike, almost at breaking point, he knew, and he felt strangely sympathetic, recognising the man fighting to get through all this.

'OK. I will, Mike. I think you can go home to the ranch next Monday—six days from today. We will have the casts off before then, but I won't know more until I've seen the X-rays. Providing there's no infection or thrombosis. . . You won't be able to put weight on those legs for weeks, so it means having someone to look after you up there. I mean, someone trained and preferably able to do a spot of therapy as well. You can have physio at your own hospital. But I'd like to see you down here occasionally, just the same.'

'I understand all that.'

'OK. I would have liked to see your case through. However, assuming that you're fit to travel, by ambulance of course, with a nurse who will have to monitor you and stay for at least three weeks, you can leave here on Monday. I will refer you to your local hospital then.'

'That's great news. Thanks.' Now Mike was looking beyond him to where Sarah stood holding his notes. 'I want Nurse Hillier.'

Neil looked at her consideringly. 'Nurse Hillier, are you willing to take this case on? I think I would be happier about the whole thing if you were to go with him.' He looked back to Mike. 'This could turn out to be rather an expensive business, you know?'

'I shan't quibble about that,' the rancher answered grimly. 'Expense is no problem fortunately. But I do have to be on the spot, Dr Patterson. I've been away too long.'

'All right, Mike. Just concentrate on getting yourself fit for the rest of the week. Relax.' He turned to Sarah. 'I'd like to see my other patients now, Nurse, while I'm here.' Glancing at his watch he hurried to the door. 'I have another consultation in fifteen minutes.'

Outside the door Neil asked softly, 'Is all this OK with you? If I go ahead and arrange it?'

'Yes. I'm quite looking forward to it now actually.' It was only when he gave her a frowning second glance that she realised what she had said. But by then she couldn't retract or explain, for he had already pushed open the door of room four. She heard him say, 'Hello, there—how are you now?' his eyes professionally searching while he reached for the notes in Sarah's hand, and Mike was eradicated from his mind temporarily.

But from then on Mike was stimulated by the decisions made and did everything he could to help his progress along. Most of his days were spent on the balcony unless he was driven in by the sudden summer storms prevalent in that part of Columbia.

On Thursday, as Sarah was just leaving, he asked for the phone to be brought to him and she wondered if he was going to call Monique. Did she know he was coming home? Would Sarah meet her there? What would it be like at the ranch? Primitive? Like the ranches she had seen in westerns—some very luxurious, some very spartan? Would he lose some of his irascibility, or perhaps the reverse—become even more demanding?

It offered quite a challenge and she had spoken the truth when she had admitted that she was looking forward to it. Because soon she would know that she had helped him through and got him once more on his feet—literally. And away from Neil maybe she would see their relationship—although it wasn't yet quite that—in perspective, and maybe he would do the same. Because, although she was almost sure of her own real and growing love for him, he seemed to be putting a brake on his own feelings now, as if he was holding back, waiting for something. But what?

At least there was their date on Saturday to look forward to, and time to talk away from the hospital.

CHAPTER NINE

By Friday another nurse had already taken over the patients in the other wards because Sarah had her own preparations to make: adequate medication and dressings; a wheelchair which could be folded and which Mike would need when he could get himself around and before he could manage on elbow crutches or even sticks. Because, for a time, it would all be down to her. She was responsible.

And that evening, as she showered, she was still turning over in her mind things like access, distance from the hospital, what it would be like so far from any other homestead, and, should an emergency arise, where did one phone?

Her own phone rang as she was wrapping herself in a bath-towel after her shower. It was Neil, explaining that he had to cancel their date for Saturday. He had been going to take her to the top of Grouse Mountain in the sky-tram and they would have had a meal up there. She had been looking forward to the view from the top.

'Instead I have to fly down to Edmonton tomorrow, to the university for a weekend seminar. Dr Hayes has had to cancel. He's gone down with a virus, so it can't be helped. It's important that one of us should be there.'

She tried not to show her disappointment, drawing in a deep breath before saying lightly, 'I understand, and there will be other times. Besides, I have quite a lot to do if I'm going into the backwoods for a few weeks.'

'Oh, of course. Monday, isn't it? I'll see him before you leave. Hopefully, I'll be back on Sunday night. If not, an early breakfast flight on Monday. Is Mike being co-operative?'

'Oh, yes. Now that he knows he's going home.'

'It's much too early, of course. But if you're there. . . We'll just have to see how it goes. This weekend has rather messed things up. I was looking forward to taking you up in the ski-lift.'

'Me, too.'

'Some other time. Bye, Sarah.'

'Goodbye,' she murmured, wrapping her towel more closely around her. Tonight he was the surgeon and she the nurse, she thought, smiling ruefully. Perhaps this was why she had reservations about getting too involved. Yet how different he could be, especially when the tender wanting note crept into his voice and his arms reached to hold her.

After all, she was going away for three weeks at the least. It was going to be a long weekend, even though she would be busy with her own preparations and packing.

On Monday Neil came striding into Mike's room, his starched white coat dazzling in the morning sun streaming in through the open window.

He bent over the bed and examined the weak muscle-slackened legs, scarred, yet healthier than he had hoped for. And throughout the whole examination Mike just grinned like a Cheshire cat.

'Yes—good. But you'll need a great deal of patience, Mike. Exercise and therapy is the next stage, and up to you. But for heaven's sake—go slowly.'

'Thanks—for everything,' he said huskily.

'OK. We'll see you some time. You'll have an outpatient's appointment in due course.'

Yesterday Joe had been requested to 'Get some of my gear down here, there's a good guy. The light blue trousers and sweater, oh—and a summer shirt. Midge will know. No—no shoes, sandals maybe, or even thick socks'.

Sarah had listened. Mike was like a child going on an outing. But she, waiting for some extra word from Neil, had been disappointed. There had been so much pressure on the surgeon this week that he simply hadn't got time, or had forgotten, before flying down to Edmonton.

But Joe must have driven down and back on Sunday evening for today, supported by pillows and strapped to his stretcher bed, Mike was wearing trousers. The pale blue sweatshirt matching his eyes, and the sweater around his shoulders improved his ego enormously as he gazed out of the window when the ambulance began the ninety-mile journey to his ranch.

Already the new life quality had infused Sarah with the same enthusiastic approach. She was so happy for him, gazing out with rapt expression at the disappearing suburbs. Out past the lumber mills, the harbour on the Fraser River, floating logs, through farm country, Dutch barns, red and white, tiny churches and scattered houses watched over by the mountains. Glimpses of the Fraser, gushing relentlessly between the canyons below, wild rugged scenery and then—Fort Langley, which, Mike told her, 'Was once a fort and trading post established in 1827. Indian country.' On through valleys and grandeur which left her breathless. But then Mike was silent. She saw him wince and his face whiten.

'Are you in pain? Is something wrong?'

He shook his head slowly. How could he tell her that they had just passed the scene of the crash?

Although Sarah was keeping a professional eye on her patient she too was excited about the whole thing. It was like going on holiday and she was really enjoying it because Mike's enthusiasm was infectious. She said this to him, her eyes reflecting her feelings, and several times after that, when she turned quickly, she found him watching her.

Her hair fascinated him. She had washed it the

previous evening and it was soft and bouncy, dancing with highlights in the sun through the long windows.

But after Chilliwack he was under pressure, finding it difficult to keep his feelings under control. His legs in the pale blue trousers looked long and lifeless. But the rest of him was very much alive.

And then Hope was signposted.

Sarah was recalling an article she had once read. 'Isn't this where the gold rush started, Mike?'

'On the Fraser—yes. In 1856. There were reputed to be ten thousand miners in this valley at that time. Right through from here to the Cariboo; must have been absolute madness. Think of the conditions, the hazards—not to mention the Indians up there on those ridges. It's seething with history—and not too much of it makes one very proud. Gold makes men behave like savages.'

'It still does, only in a more subtle way. At least, on the surface,' she murmured.

He was watching her carefully. 'In other words, money and possessions aren't the first priority with you, Sarah.'

'No, Mike. I don't think they are. And I imagine most people who work in hospitals feel the same.'

'You could be right at that,' he said thoughtfully. 'My mother feels like you and she certainly didn't have it easy. She had to stock up for six months at a time, do all her own baking and freezing. Milk and beef were here, of course, only now there are food freezers and I generate my own power and purify my water from the streams.'

'Good heavens! Do you really?'

'Sure. It comes down from the hills and through one of the fields and it's then piped to the house.'

She hadn't realised that his lifestyle was quite so spartan. 'What happens if it dries up?'

'Oh. . .' he laughed '. . .it isn't that primitive. It never has dried up. Initially it's fed by the snow in the

spring run-off—that's when the snow on the mountains
starts to melt. You can hear the rumble and movement
as if the whole of nature is waking up after the winter.
One day—a kind of stillness because there's snow
everywhere, and then suddenly everything starts to
move and the run-off begins. Will you tell the driver to
turn off at the next exit?'

She tapped the glass panel dividing them and he
nodded without turning his head.

Now the road became a track, though quite wide
enough for a car. There were horses' hoof-marks in the
muddy edges and, after ten minutes or so, Mike leaned
forward in anticipation. To the right of them an arrow
pointed to the Rayner Ranch. They turned off and
soon drove under an archway. This then was his ranch.
About a mile further on, as they rounded a bend, the
house was in sight. It was surrounded by a white ranch
fence. Sarah saw horses huddled together in the corral,
and cattle in fields with no fencing because they
stretched away into eternity it seemed.

The house was larger than she had expected, all the
rooms being on one floor. A veranda went all round
the outside. The huge logs were criss-crossed at the
corners in true homestead style and the roof, made of
wood tiles, coming well out over the windows so the
snow could slide off and miss them. The heavy door
stood open as the ambulance drew up at the veranda
steps.

Joe and his wife Midge, a woman in her forties whom
Sarah liked at once, were waiting. Two cowhands came
from the cattle sheds and still two more from behind
the stables, running across the gravel to wave their
stetsons above their heads, as Sarah got down first.

Then through the open doorway came Monique,
looking at the scene in front of her.

'Quite a homecoming,' Sarah observed to the man
on the bed-stretcher who was grinning delightedly and
hadn't yet seen her. She hadn't expected Monique to

be there for some reason, and there was a definite lowering of her spirits in consequence.

And now Mike, too, was looking a little disconcerted, even frowning, and so soon after the sheer pleasure which had lit up his face a moment ago. Sarah busied herself with collecting his things together.

'The guys will see to all that,' Mike told her as Joe approached.

'Hello, Joe,' she said with her attractive smile. 'I've brought him home, you see.'

'And right glad we are to see him, Nurse—that's for sure. Now—how do we get him up those steps?'

'I suggest he stays on the stretcher. It can be wheeled and then lifted up on to the veranda. I don't want to disturb his legs too suddenly.'

Monique had come slowly over to the ambulance. Her first words made Sarah's hackles rise.

'Hi, there—journey's end, Mike. But surely you aren't going to let them carry you in on that thing, are you? What's the matter with your legs? The plasters are off, aren't they? You can walk. . .?'

Sarah ignored her.

Mike simply said, 'Hello, Monique. I didn't expect you to be here.' Then he looked at Sarah and gave her a mischievous grin. 'Well, Nurse? Shall I try walking in?'

'You will definitely not,' she said firmly, and walked beside him while he was wheeled across the veranda and into a large room which was obviously lived-in.

'Through to the bedroom?' Joe asked.

'No thanks, Joe,' his boss answered at once. 'Over there on the chesterfield, I think. And for God's sake, open up the windows.'

'Your temper hasn't improved.' Monique spoke from the doorway.

'Why did *you* come over here?' Mike said, looking up at her. 'Not for any good reason apparently.'

'Oh—just to make sure that Midge had cleaned

through properly,' she said glibly. 'Besides, it's different now the boss is back. . .' She tossed back her black hair over a white-sweatered shoulder. Then her eyes opened even wider and her expression changed as one of the cowhands came in with Sarah's two bags and deposited them on to the floor. 'What are those for? You're not staying here, surely?' she asked Sarah, her eyes flashing dangerously as the two girls faced each other.

'I'm afraid there is no alternative,' Sarah said clearly in her best English accent. 'I'm here on Dr Patterson's instructions and at Mr Rayner's request. Now—could someone show me his bedroom so that I can get his medical things unpacked?'

Midge came forward. 'It's this way, Nurse,' she said quietly.

In his room a wide window looked across the ranges. The walls were white with the original wood beams. The bed was covered with a deep maroon spread to match the curtains and there were green patterned rugs on the dark wood floor.

'It smells nice—you've been polishing,' Sarah said at once. 'It's lovely, Midge, if I can call you that.'

'Yes, Nurse.'

'Oh—Sarah, please. We'll have a talk when I've got Mr Rayner settled. Perhaps you could show me where I'm to sleep and I'll get rid of these bags.'

'It's right next door. The boss had it redecorated last year. It's a nice room.'

'Yes. It is.' Sarah was surprised at the charming room which was to be hers. Here too the roof was beamed, the walls were white but with pale blue linen curtains and spread. A deeper blue carpet covered the centre and the floors were dark wood and polished. An armchair was upholstered in pale green and edged with blue, as was the bedside lamp. She hadn't expected anything like this. Was it for Monique's benefit? Did she sleep in here sometimes? she wondered.

Sarah washed her hands and ran a comb through her hair, deliberately pinning a cap on her head, mainly for Monique's benefit and to maintain her professional status. She felt it might be necessary.

In the kitchen was another pleasant surprise: Midge was setting out the coffee-mugs and the ambulance driver was tucking into lunch on a tray.

In the living-room Mike and Joe were talking together. Monique was down by the corral looking at the horses. Sarah went back to the kitchen to see if she could help.

'No, thank you,' Midge told her. 'I've made a fresh salmon salad for you and the boss. It's one of his favourites and, as it's late, I thought chicken for tonight. I always come in and cook for him.'

'And do the house?'

'Yes. I had a baking day yesterday so there's a good stock of bread in the freezer. Oh, it is good to have him back. How is he?'

'Doing very well. But he must take it slowly. We don't want any setbacks. So if he is too adventurous I shall no doubt bully him a little. He wanted to get home so desperately, Midge.'

'Well—there were a few problems which Joe couldn't very well cope with. But on the whole it's running smoothly enough. It's been a worry to Joe, though. There have been upsets and the men don't like that. Neither will they take orders from a woman.'

'I—understand that. If it's ready I'll take it along to him. He can manage it on a tray now.'

Joe and Mike had finished their conversation for the time being and Mike had his head back on the pillow Sarah had brought in earlier. He looked tired but that was a normal reaction after the journey and trauma of his homecoming. Besides, he was wondering what Monique was up to.

She began walking back to the house when she saw Joe leave and now came very positively into the room, the white cotton sweater a perfect foil for her colouring. She lifted her arms which emphasised her voluptuous figure, sweeping her hair up from her neck in an abandoned gesture as she threw herself into a chair, ignoring Sarah. Mike watched her.

'So, Mike, what gives? Are you pleased to see me? You haven't shown it yet.'

'Sure I'm glad to see you, Monique. I've missed you. I just didn't expect you to be here after the way you've neglected me these last weeks.'

'Oh, you know me, honey. I run a mile from anything to do with hospitals. I came over to lunch with you but it's a bit late for that now.'

Because she would be watching him Mike would not enjoy his meal at all, Sarah knew instinctively. Any weakness would be highlighted and he would hate that. But he looked up at her. 'Will you ask Midge to rustle up another lunch, Sarah?'

'Yes. Of course.'

'And bring yours in here too.'

'Oh—I can eat in the kitchen. I'm sure you have a lot to talk about.'

She left before he could protest but as Monique did not keep her voice lowered she couldn't not hear her surprised comment. 'So she's Sarah, is she? Going to be very cosy for you, isn't it, darling?'

'Monique, behave!' he said curtly.

But Sarah, enjoying her meal alone in the kitchen after the ambulance driver had gone, found her mind occupied with a great deal of conflicting thoughts. Until Midge came back to do the dishes and she went into Mike's room to get his medication.

As she administered it, Monique watched with a half-smile which Sarah found irritating, but her patient was her first concern.

'I think you should rest now,' she told him.

'Oh—I have to go anyway. I have a fishing party

coming in for a meal at six, as well as casuals off the lake.' Monique pushed her plate away.

'The restaurant is going well, then?' Mike commented.

'Oh, sure. I knew it would once I had it organised.'

Mike caught Sarah's eye—she was sure she saw a mischievous glint in his when he said lightly, 'I'll bring Sarah over as soon as I'm mobile. Joe can drive us. Wonder how soon I can make it?'

'Really!' Monique almost exploded, throwing her head back like a mare scenting danger before crossing the room to the chesterfield. 'And when are you going to shave off that nauseating beard?'

He smoothed his face, keeping his temper in check. 'I've grown rather attached to it. No one else seems to object.'

'Well,' she assured him, 'I do. So don't expect me to get near you until it's gone, Mike. And I mean that. . .'

'You're not going off me—surely?' His eyes were dangerously narrowed.

'Slowly and surely. . .' she threw back over her shoulder as she went out through the door.

Mike's chin went up. Sarah knew he was hurt. They both heard her car rev up and whiz down the drive. She went along to his room and left him to his thoughts which were just a little despairing at that moment.

When she went back twenty minutes later he didn't remonstrate at her insistence that he got some rest while she finished unpacking for them both.

His bedroom contained some very solid colonial furniture and she felt a little strange, here among his personal possessions. He became more the man than the patient somehow.

She felt the bed. It was firm and resilient.

Midge spoke from the doorway. 'Is everything all right?'

'Fine. Maybe some more pillows?' she suggested.

When Midge brought them she stood in the doorway

and watched Sarah. 'The boss isn't going to like staying indoors now he's back here,' she confided. 'Out there with his cattle from dawn to dusk usually. This happened so suddenly. It was a shock and a big headache for Joe. But it's good to have him home. When do you think he'll be getting out there?'

'Certainly not until he's more mobile. We dare not risk another injury: a fall or anything like that. I've brought a folding chair for him but he isn't going to like it a bit. But it does mean that when he has more balance he can manoeuvre himself—to the bathroom, for instance. And on to the veranda if someone is with him. He could see what is going on from there, couldn't he?'

Midge said, 'Knowing him, he will already have worked that out for himself. But I quite thought his parents would have flown over. Joe and I would have liked that, I guess.'

'They haven't yet been told.'

'Is that right?' Midge was obviously surprised.

'Mike didn't want to worry them.'

'They're not going to like being kept in the dark. Although they know how independent he is, I guess. What time do you want supper?'

'Around six-thirty, if that's all right. It's the time he has been eating in hospital. And then he should have an early night. It was a very long journey.'

'Does he do what you say all the time?' Midge asked in an awed voice.

Sarah smiled. 'Usually. But not for much longer, I'm sure. I'll go and see if he is awake.'

He was and sitting upright on the chesterfield, with both blue-clad legs dangling and his bare feet resting on the floor.

'What on earth are you doing?' She hurried across the room to him.

'Don't panic. Is Joe around?' he asked calmly,

ignoring her question. 'If so—ask him to come here. Or one of the others.'

'Is it urgent, Mike?'

'Very.'

Midge, right behind Sarah, went to call Joe.

He came at once. 'What's the trouble?' He looked from one to the other.

Mike answered, 'No trouble, Joe. Just give me a hand into this chair. You can come with me just this once, if you like.'

And so a new order of things began as Mike took himself to the bathroom for the first time since the accident. And in doing so recaptured his male image.

Except later when he said suddenly, 'She didn't call, did she?'

'Monique?'

He nodded. 'Can't blame her, I guess. What girl in their right senses would want a guy who looks as I do? I can't even stand on my own two feet.'

'Don't be so depressed,' said Sarah, her voice a little husky, which she countered by giving the pillows on his bed a good shake and pushing them down into his back. 'Every day is going to show a difference. Your own doggedness will get you up in the saddle again. A few broken bones don't make you any less a man, Mike. You're not fully recovered. It just needs time and perseverance. She'll wait.'

His blue eyes were bright in the evening light, almost startlingly so, as he looked straight at her unflinchingly. 'I'm damaged goods, Sarah. You're the one who's been putting the pieces back together—so you should know. What do *you* think of me?'

'Mike Rayner—don't feel so sorry for yourself. To me you are very much a man and I don't feel in the least sorry for you—there's no need. The worst is over now.' It was the best she could do to eliminate his depression.

'Your opinion isn't shared by Monique, obviously,' he said bitterly.

'Oh, she's just a little out of touch and doesn't like to see you—changed. But—it will soon be all right again.'

'Will it? I wonder.'

'Of course,' she continued, her voice deliberately light. 'You'll be getting back to work now—the paperwork, that is. The rest is up to you and me—and your physiotherapist. Now, what about a few exercises if you feel up to it?'

'Breaking me in?'

'Slowly. Raise your left leg—stretch your toes. Gently, Mike. . .'

They ended by laughing over that first tentative toe-wagging, which she did with him to show which movements would have the best results. She also noted where it still hurt, which movements he avoided and where there was most weakness.

But once he was in bed, the soft glow of his bedside lamp casting shadows across the room, she too relaxed. Outside the unaccustomed sounds of night shut them into the quiet of his home. She left him then, pausing at the door to extract his promise that he would call her if he needed anything.

'Don't attempt to get out of bed by yourself, Mike,' she said seriously. 'You could land yourself back in hospital.'

'OK,' he promised, reluctantly, 'but it won't be too long before I'm mobile.'

'I'm sure it won't. Goodnight.'

After her shower, feeling fresh and restored, she pulled the belt of her housecoat around her waist and, going to make sure that the heavy door was locked— which it wasn't, probably because Mike never bothered so didn't tell her—she put out the lights and then looked around Mike's bedroom door. He was still awake. 'Everything all right?'

'Sure. I'll read a bit longer, I think.'

'Your tablets are still there.'

'I know. I don't know if I'll take them tonight.'

'It's up to you now, Mike.'

'Yes. Do you have all you need?'

'Oh, yes. I feel like an honoured guest.'

'You are. And thanks for coming back here with me. Although I guess I would have made it, it's great to know you're next door.'

'What a nice thing to say. But I do know what you mean. All patients feel the same way the first night at home, not having the night staff around, or a doctor on call if anything goes wrong. But nothing can, unless you become too adventurous.'

He said coolly, 'Unfortunately, my nocturnal adventures are rather curtailed right now.'

She was drawn to meet his intensely probing blue eyes. He knew exactly what he was saying.

She left him with a firm, 'Goodnight.'

Next morning Sarah woke at six and gave herself a luxurious ten minutes while she looked around her room and planned her working day, which would depend very much on Mike and what he had in mind.

Except for her cap she meticulously dressed in her uniform before taking his orange juice in to him. He had heard her in the kitchen and was watching the door.

'Hi.' He pulled himself up in bed.

'Good morning. Did you sleep well?' she asked.

'I guess so. It's raining.'

'Yes.'

'I wanted to get out and take a look around.'

'Maybe later.'

'Anything wrong, Sarah? No lovely smile for your patient today?'

'Open your mouth. . .'

She popped the thermometer in. Now it was safe to

smile at him. Or was it? Because he was watching her movements too intently. She put out the clothes he wanted. Was she going to have problems with him? Surely not? She had thought Monique might have taken care of that side of things.

Neil phoned quite early before he left for the hospital. Her heart lightened at the sound of his voice, even though they only discussed their patient.

'Well done,' he ended. 'We're missing you already.'

'I'm glad you said that,' she said softly, but noticing that he said 'we' instead of 'I'.

By afternoon the sky had cleared to an azure blue. The sweet smell of wild flowers drifted from the meadows and a yellow carpet of them covered the foothills. Mike was out there propelling himself around the cattle pens, inspecting those which Joe had chosen for the sale ring.

'That little lot should keep the bank manager happy. They're first class, Joe. You've got the trucks laid on?'

'They sure are, boss. I told you there was no need to worry on my account.'

'Except that you were up here working yourself to a cinder. And not being left to do it your own way. I'm sorry about that.'

'No harm done. It was best to get some kind of understanding.'

Sarah wondered what would happen when Monique came to live here permanently. Surely some sparks would fly then. But it was not her concern, she reminded herself.

Mike was looking towards the corral. 'Where's Hamlet, Joe?'

'Down in the long field. Having himself a roll in a bed of clover from what I can see. He doesn't know you're back yet.'

'Get him up here. I'd—like to see him.'

'Sure, boss. And I'll come up to the house with the books presently, if you're free.'

'I'm not going any place; but make it before supper.'

Three heads turned as a small red car sped up the drive between the white-painted fences and stopped. Monique got out and slammed the door, coming towards them with swinging hips.

'Hi, there.'

She was wearing a yellow bikini top and white shorts. Her legs were superb, Sarah had to admit, as was her figure. Both men looked at her appreciatively. Mike said, 'Hi,' as she came closer, while Sarah quietly excused herself. She didn't want a repetition of yesterday.

Instead of going back into the house, she wandered down towards the meadows and along the banks of a stream rushing with clear water over the stones, lost in the fresh beauty and quiet around her. The cattle were grazing over a large area, adding to the authenticity of the scene; there were far more than she had imagined.

When she heard Joe's voice calling, and turned back, she hadn't realised how far she had come. Her thoughts went immediately to Mike as Joe came galloping towards her over the grass.

'What's happened, Joe? Something wrong?'

'It's you, Nurse. Those bulls over there—not very social. In fact darned dangerous if they rushed you.'

'I'm not scared of them. Why are they separated from the rest of the cattle?'

'To keep them away from the cows,' he told her bluntly.

'Oh—how stupid of me. No wonder they're cross— just looking at them through a hedge. I didn't realise. I'm sorry.'

'The boss sent me after you when you went out of sight. He's worried about you.'

CHAPTER TEN

'I DIDN'T know I'd come so far,' Sarah confessed.

Joe eyed her speculatively. 'If you can get up behind me, I'll give you a ride back.'

Her sense of fun was evident. 'Oh, yes—wait for it. . .'

Joe swung her up behind him, obviously enjoying it too, his weather-tanned face under the stetson hat one enormous grin as he trotted back with Sarah's arms around his waist, she looking flushed and penitent as they approached the two onlookers, her hair blowing out behind her.

Mike's concern hadn't escaped Monique's keen eyes. Her expression was anything but amused and she couldn't resist a snide remark. 'I thought you were here to look after your patient, Nurse, or is it the reverse? In which case he doesn't need you.'

Sarah ignored her, going instead to Mike who looked pale and tense. 'I am very sorry. I—didn't think——'

'Don't ever do that to me again,' he said abruptly. 'You are never to go off on your own anywhere up here. They could have stampeded and they're bad-tempered at that.'

It was all eased by Midge calling from the veranda that the local hospital was on the phone. 'For Nurse Hillier.'

It was a Miss Turner to arrange Mike's physio-therapy. Under the present circumstances she agreed to come out to the ranch every day until he was able to attend her clinic.

'So you do have all Mr Rayner's notes, Miss Turner?'

'Yes. I spoke to Dr Patterson on the phone. He sent them up by mail coach.'

144

'Fine. We'll see you tomorrow, then.'

Their voices outside on the veranda meant that Mike was back there. Sarah found him looking hot and restless in his chair, and obviously waiting for her to reappear.

'Was that Dr Patterson?' he asked quickly.

'No. The physiotherapist. She's coming over tomorrow.'

'Oh.'

Monique was lying outstretched on a lounge-chair, smoking, watching the rings being absorbed into the air.

'Can I get you something? Tea, coffee or lemonade? I've made some with fresh lemons,' Sarah suggested.

Mike's face relaxed. 'Oh, Sarah—yes. Monique?'

'Coffee for me. Black—no sugar.'

When she carried out the tray Monique was telling him about the apparent success of the improvements she had made.

'Two new fishing boats for the lake. And the trailer park is full every night.'

'So you wouldn't have had time to spare if the dude idea had gone ahead,' Mike said in the low-pitched voice Sarah admired. 'How did you think it could work?'

Monique didn't reply, reaching for her coffee, pointedly ignoring Sarah who put the jug of iced lemon down on to the rough-hewn pine table beside Mike and left them.

There was a strained look on his face now which her trained eyes had detected at once. Probably his legs were aching, stiff from the position they were in. But he wouldn't thank Sarah for intruding if she suggested a move. Perhaps Monique would be leaving soon, she thought anxiously. They weren't exactly behaving like lovers.

When her car eventually revved up and the engine grew fainter, Sarah went to him. Her soft shoes on the wood flooring made no noise. He didn't hear her. But she saw that he was leaning forward, staring out across the cattle-scattered ranges, deep in thought. Then he tried to lift each leg in turn and his arm, wincing because of the weak muscles, still at the aching stage, as he tried once more to flex his leg.

'Damn. . .' he groaned. 'Oh—what the hell?'

Sarah stepped back and this time deliberately made more noise as she approached. His expression changed at once. 'Don't you think you should lie down for a bit?' she suggested.

Turning his chair himself, he propelled it into the house, cooler than outside, stopping to say, 'Why don't we have that chesterfield nearer the window? What do you think?'

'Why not? I'll move it there now. It runs easily.'

The room looked quite different as she put his table beside him and got him settled on the long settee. He smiled gratefully, making no further attempt to hide his lethargy from her as he reached for some magazines, turning to tell her that, 'Joe is coming over to go through a few things with me. So why don't you take some free time and find those books you wanted? They're on that second shelf. Unless you've something else in mind, such as running wild among the cowslips. . .?'

'Oh, don't remind me!' She met the teasing blue eyes raised to hers, one of his rare grins sending her spirits soaring. He had strong white teeth, and in full health would be a dream of a man if one was attracted to the earthy type. And most girls would be. Even she was very aware of his male magnetism.

But it was love—something else—which she wanted from Neil. A deeper, more enveloping attraction which, as yet, she couldn't express, was a part of her need to be with him as often as possible.

Armed with three books on British Columbia's history, Sarah forgot everything, immersed in the struggles of those early pioneers.

Next evening Neil phoned again. 'Hello, Sarah. How are you?'

'I'm fine. I wasn't expecting you to——'

'And our rancher?'

'He's out on the veranda. The physio went quite well this morning. Fortunately he quite likes Janet Turner. She seems very professional.'

'She is. I know her quite well.'

'I see.'

'No, you don't. Not that well. But how are you really coping up there among the natives?'

'I'm enjoying it. But I am missing the hospital routine.'

'And me?' He waited.

'And you. . .' she said softly.

'Call me at home some time,' he concluded, and she heard voices in the background and guessed he was in his consulting-room. 'I've two agency nurses starting tomorrow. We are very pressurised: so many tourists in town. No let-up this week at all. Call me, after nine some time, Sarah. I'm here until eight most nights this week.'

She promised that she would, aware of a new inflexion in his voice tonight. Then she went to tell Mike that Neil had phoned.

He said, after a pause, 'I suppose he wants you down there—is that it?'

'He did say they are terribly busy at the hospital, but it will depend on your progress when I go back.'

He raised his eyebrows but made no further comment, and she leaned on the fence and admired the black stallion which came over immediately when Mike said authoritatively, 'Hamlet—here, boy!'

* * *

Next morning Sarah went to the bathroom to help Mike manoeuvre his chair back to his bedroom, and stopped in the doorway. He was watching closely to see her reaction. His beard had been shaved off.

'Well—is it an improvement?' he asked drily, though she sensed his eagerness as his eyes searched hers.

'I had no idea you were so good-looking. It's marvellous! How did your arm stand up to it?'

'Not badly. I'm winning, Sarah. Now for these.' He looked down at his legs while she wheeled him out.

'Perhaps your physio will try you with crutches soon, Mike.' She looked closer. 'Your scars are fading, aren't they?'

He grinned. 'It's great. Now—if you'll buzz off I'll get into my trousers.' He was already peeling off his blue towelling robe, his bare chest accentuating his renewed male figure and she went out quickly.

In the bathroom the scent of his aftershave still hung in the steamy air. Sarah was glad to be alone for a moment while she got her thoughts into line. The patient was fast disappearing and the man emerging and Mike, in any relationship, would be the dominant male. As she picked up his towels and put away his shaver, she wondered what Monique's reaction would be when she saw him without the beard she disliked so much. Was that why he had taken it off?

But Monique had still not been out to the ranch since that day on the veranda, when something had transpired which had sent her off in a rage and made Mike curse. To Sarah it was a relief that she stayed away, but it didn't remove her image or the impression that she and Mike had obviously had a very strong sexual relationship. She knew this because Monique made no secret of the fact that they were lovers.

Almost two weeks later his progress had continued and it was arranged that next day they would drive into Hope to the physiotherapist instead of her coming out to the ranch. Mike had taken his first tentative steps

with the aid of crutches, and later Sarah was going to
call Neil and tell him of this new positive progress. In
any case he had promised to drive up himself on
Sunday.

Now she went to make coffee in the kitchen and, on
going back into the sitting-room, she saw Mike on his
feet, leaning against the end of the chesterfield, supported only by his hands, unable to move. When he
swayed she put down the tray and flew across the room,
holding him around his waist from behind.

'Try to turn around,' she said firmly. And he did,
very slowly, into her arms. For a split second he
hesitated, then, with a low groan, his hands moved to
the small of her back and he was straining her to his
questing body, his face coming down to hers, searching
for her mouth.

She knew his desperate need but this was
unacceptable.

'This is just not on, Mike. . .' she said, pitting her
strength against his as she forced him back against the
end of the settee, putting some space between them
now. His breath was expelled then in a different groan
as he tried to move his leg. Immediately she was alert,
reaching for his crutch. 'Hold on to me, Mike——'

'No,' he said thickly, pushing her away. 'I'll do it
myself.'

She watched him painfully lower himself on to the
settee, then reached to switch on the light beside him,
enclosing them both in a deceptively warm glow. 'Now
tell me, where is the pain?'

'Just—go away, Sarah. Just go,' he told her
wretchedly. 'You must have seen that coming, and
don't tell me you didn't because I know differently.'

Because she could no longer bear to stay in the room
she picked up the coffee-tray and went out to the
kitchen, automatically switching on to make a fresh
pot. Anger and a deep hurt had taken over. She felt
stunned and shocked by his reactions, as if she were to

blame. Her hands were still trembling as she stared unseeingly across the kitchen, out to where the sky was deepening into night. She would have liked to walk away, never to see that disparaging expression on his face again. But neither could she go to bed and leave him to fend for himself. So when the coffee was ready, gathering all the shreds of dignity she could muster, she went back into the softly lit room.

He was reading, so she put the tray down beside him and turned to go. He looked up, reaching himself for the blue mountain pottery pot. 'Black or white, Sarah? I'm sorry, I guess. That was unforgivable. Forget it. Have yours with me.'

She took her cup from him, making her eyes meet his. 'I can't do that, Mike—forget it happened. Perhaps you're right: it is time for me to leave. Will you phone Dr Patterson, please?'

'No. He wouldn't be at the hospital this late and I don't have his home number.'

'Then perhaps in the morning you might reach him through his secretary,' she said coolly.

'Sarah—I've said I'm sorry. What more do you want?'

'Nothing. Just to be able to resume my normal duties at the hospital as soon as possible.'

He looked at her for a long moment before saying tersely, 'I can get myself to bed. No need for you to hang around.'

'Right. Goodnight, then.'

She left him then, but knowing she wouldn't be able to relax until he was safely in bed—and not even then, unless the ache in her throat, along all her nerve-ends, began to subside a little. But at last the house was silent, his light switched off.

Next morning Neil's secretary phoned Sarah, and a moment later the surgeon's voice came over the wires, clinching her return.

'Sarah—Mike has called me. What do you think

about coming back?' he asked at once. 'Is he ready to be left yet? He seems to think so.'

She told him that both she and Mike felt he could manage after the weekend.

'So, how will you travel? Train, coach?'

She hadn't considered that. 'I'm not sure. . .'

'So why don't I drive up as arranged? What about this Sunday? Is that too soon?'

'No—that would be fine. And he could always have someone in from here to help.'

'Yes. Good. We're a bit thin on the ground with qualified people at the hospital right now, and I gather that Mike is well on the mend. That's what he says. . .'

'Yes. Yes, he is.'

'Good. Sunday, then. Look forward to that.'

She broke the news to Mike as they prepared to leave for his treatment. Outside a yellow Buick stood at the veranda steps. Surprised, because she didn't know he owned a car like that, Sarah was however feeling too dejected to bother about such mundane things, except to register that Mike would find it more comfortable than the Land Rover.

Now his clear direct eyes met hers before he had time to hide his dismay. 'This Sunday? Isn't that a bit soon?'

She nodded. 'It was your suggestion. But you don't really need me now and there are others who do.'

'Dr Patterson takes priority, naturally——'

'He has a new intake on Monday.' She made herself ignore his reference to Neil personally.

'OK. . .' He was staring at the floor.

'It—gives us a few more days,' she began. 'I want to be sure you——'

'There's no need. I'm over the worst. I'm OK.'

'I know. But it will be quite a while before you can get back to real work, Mike.'

'Obviously. I'm not a complete idiot. . .' he gave her a rueful smile '. . .though you probably don't agree.'

She went to the open door, watching Joe coming across from the stables to collect them. She couldn't joke about yesterday. Not yet. The hurt was still there.

'Tell Joe to wait,' he said suddenly. 'I want to talk to Monique. She'll probably be over, now that she knows you're going.'

'Is that why she hasn't. . .?' she began incredulously.

'I guess so.'

Quietly she went on through and across the wooden floor, passing on his message to Joe waiting beside the huge gleaming car.

She heard Mike call her and went back into the room swiftly. Anything could have happened. Nothing had. Instead he was attempting to get co-ordinated with his crutches, his blue cotton shirt open at the neck, showing his strong chest and sleek waist, belted into blue jeans, standing tall and straight, blue eyes coolly appraising Sarah as she rushed in.

'Oh—I thought——'

'Full marks, Sarah. I knew I'd make it in under three weeks! And to celebrate the fact that I'm back in circulation we're going over to the Boat-house on Saturday for a meal. I've just talked to Monique.'

She attempted to hide her relief that they were once again on normal terms by saying, 'And what did she say to that?'

'Why should she say anything? I just said we wanted a table. Don't you want to go out with me? It will be the first and last time.' He grinned. 'You're not sure of our reception. Is that it? Not to worry on that score. Everything will be fine. She knows it's your last night here—and. . .' he grinned wickedly '. . . I'm minus my beard—remember? I know Monique of old. . .'

In the car, from the front seat where he insisted on sitting, Mike asked over his shoulder, 'How are you getting back to Vancouver on Sunday?'

Sarah told him that Neil was driving up to the ranch to collect her.

'Yes. I thought he might do that. You and he have something going, don't you?'

When Sarah didn't answer, he made no further comment. She just knew that she could barely wait until she was with Neil again. She knew every part of his face, every line, the way his hair grew, low on his forehead; and his eyes, changing according to his mood or the situation: thoughtful, concerned, assertive or simply expressive when he was about to kiss her and they became eloquent with desire. And, oh—how she was longing until they were together again.

It would be really nice to be with him all the way back to Vancouver.

Saturday arrived. Midge came up while Sarah sat in the lounge-chair lost in thoughts. 'I don't need to do a meal for tonight, then? Is that right, Nurse?'

'No, Midge. We're going to the Boat-house.'

'I'm glad. Joe is going to take you over there. The boss wanted to drive you himself but——'

'Oh, he isn't ready for that yet,' she said decidedly. 'Somehow, you and Joe are going to have to keep an eye on him. Whatever happens, he mustn't miss his physio for a while yet.'

'He is sure going to miss you—though he may not realise it. But we'll do our best for him, you know that.'

Later, she held her breath when Mike came out himself and manipulated the steps down from the wooden veranda, limping off in the direction of the corral with a set face and very real determination, disregarding any pain he might feel. His orange and brown cowboy shirt was open to the waist, the cream stetson on the back of his head. His high leather boots were still waiting behind the door of his bedroom, although Sarah had a suspicion that they had been tried and the discovery made that these were out of the question—as yet.

Her bags were almost ready so she decided to have a leisurely bath and take time to get ready, giving him the shower to himself.

This he could manage but it was still too difficult to get into a bath.

Punctually at seven-thirty he emerged from his room. 'I shall be the only one in a suit, I guess. But I knew you would wear a dress, so. . .' His eyes swept over Sarah's pale yellow patterned Liberty tana lawn, a present from her father, the white strapped sandals and bag to match. She knew he noticed the care she had taken.

'In that case, we'll both do very nicely,' she said, accepting the sherry he had poured for her.

The lakeside was as busy as a village. Log cabins lined the shores and continued under the trees, and trailers each had their own barbecue grid. Piles of logs were stacked ready, the smell of charcoal and steaks mingled, boats were drawn up to the landing stage, and when Joe stopped the car, away to the corner of the lake—which to Sarah seemed more like a wide endless river—could be seen a tiered wooden lodge jutting out over the water, which was Monique's home. The restaurant had been added so that, once on board, there was an illusion of being on a boat deck.

She wanted to help Mike with his sticks but she knew she didn't dare. Her heart thumped unevenly as they went in through the door beneath strings of coloured lights.

Sarah saw Monique at once. She was at the bar, glass in hand, laughing with her companion, a man wearing white trousers and a black and white striped shirt who was perched on the stool next to her.

When Monique saw them as they were being shown to their table, her expression changed. She put her hand on his arm, excusing herself, coming towards them. Her white lacy top was very low-cut, her black trousers very close-fitting, her earrings large and eye-catching. Sarah saw all this in one look, but now she was more concerned with Mike's slow progress between the tables.

When Monique reached them she said in a surprised voice, 'Hi, Mike. That was quite an entrance. You should have warned me.'

'Good evening, Monique.' Mike was very confident now that he had made it. 'What should I have warned you about?'

'You're—almost back to normal. You look—amazing.'

'Thanks. So do you. And very successful too.' He glanced round at the décor, in contrast to the more casual holiday atmosphere outside. 'Congratulations—I had no idea your plans were so ambitious. I'm glad we came. Sit here, Sarah. . .'

When he had settled his sticks to his satisfaction, he too sat down. 'I see we have a table for four,' he observed.

'Yes.' Monique looked down into his face. 'You don't mind? I thought I would have dinner with you and I'd like you to meet someone. He's here from Kamloops—for the weekend.'

Very clever, Sarah decided, while Mike too was on guard. He said, 'Oh—sure. Bring him over, and Martinis with ice and lemon for us too, please, Monique.'

So far Monique had not spoken to Sarah. And now, without a backward glance, she threaded her way back to the bar, returning with the man to whom she had been talking.

He was good-looking in a virile way, with a kind of heavy, lived-in face and eyes which swept over Sarah in an all-seeing glance when Monique introduced them.

'Dale Furnham—Mike Rayner.'

'I've heard about you,' Dale said at once. 'Glad to

know you.' His eyes went to Sarah. 'And who is this charming lady?'

'Sarah Hillier,' Mike said quietly, 'and I'm glad you think she's charming, because so do I.' Immediately he turned to look at Monique, her eyes black and shining. 'Well—as you see—I'm back on the scene again.'

'I admit I didn't ever expect to see you looking like this, Mike,' she confessed. 'How long before you're in the saddle?'

Sarah held her breath. How utterly thoughtless could one get?

'Progress in that direction is a little unpredictable just yet,' he said, smiling at her over the top of his glass. The other two, drinking bourbon, had sat down now.

Dale asked how Sarah liked Vancouver, and then Monique couldn't resist adding, 'So—it's back to that hospital for you tomorrow, is it? Ugh. . .'

'Yes. It is.'

'Are you driving down?'

'No,' Mike intervened. 'Dr Patterson is coming to collect her. I guess he feels I've borrowed her for long enough.'

Monique laughed softly. 'So, after a whole month away, that should be some reunion, I guess.'

Sarah was angry with Mike for starting this thing, wanting to defend herself.

'It isn't quite like that,' she said clearly in her very English accent. 'He has a new intake of patients for me on Monday. Besides, I've been away long enough.'

'Almost worth being ill for,' Dale chuckled, his foot tapping hers under the table. 'You're a damned lucky guy, Mike, having her all to yourself up there in the sticks—almost a month, was it?'

'I think,' Mike said dangerously, 'that we would like to order. Sarah—have you decided?'

She looked up from the menu. 'I would like the fresh salmon, I think, Mike, please.'

'Right. And now the wine.'

After that everything got better. Monique mellowed and Dale was an entertaining fourth, and the food was excellent. Sarah had never seen such a presentation accompanying the salmon, which Mike also chose. He was enjoying himself, so her scruples slipped away too. Besides, she was intrigued by Monique and her outgoing male and wondered why she had brought him to meet Mike. Unless it was deliberate: the way her mind worked.

It was Mike who decided that they should leave immediately after their coffee and liqueurs. He had been sitting for long enough. Monique had been called away, busy now as the place filled up, and Dale had taken himself off to the bar. But Monique did come over when she saw they were leaving. She looked flushed and exhilarated.

'Bye, Mike. I'll call you,' she promised.

'OK. It was a great meal, Monique. We both thought so—most enjoyable.'

Sarah smiled and went on ahead. She didn't feel—even for his sake—that she had anything further to say to Monique.

Joe was waiting with the car and she let him settle Mike inside.

'You know—I am feeling really good,' he told them. 'You enjoyed it, Sarah?'

'Very much. It was quite a surprising evening.'

'Ah—surprise is the key element, I find. It gives life an occasional fillip—and sometimes it enables one to get a few things into perspective. A very satisfactory evening, I feel. Because of you, Sarah.'

'You,' she said wonderingly, 'are talking in riddles. I'm not sure I should have had that last cognac, either. But don't you mind,' she asked seriously, 'that someone else was with your fiancée tonight? Is Dale a close friend?'

She saw his mouth tighten, and then looked away

across the brushland stretching to the foothills. It wasn't completely dark and the hills and mountains away to the right were like dark drawings against the purple-black sky.

'I'm sorry,' she murmured, contrite now. 'I shouldn't have asked that.'

'No. You shouldn't,' he said, frowning at her.

She stared back at the sombre mountains, suddenly lonely for the people she had known and loved, and homesickness returned once more.

Mike turned to give her a swift assessing glance, but didn't say anything. In fact neither of them spoke again until Joe had helped him into the house and gone to put the car away.

It was a velvety night and Sarah stood for a moment looking across to the foothills and etched mountains. Mike went straight to his room. When she knocked and went in he was pulling off his shirt.

'Bed this early was not quite what I had in mind,' he said grimly, 'but it's logical, I guess. My leg—is giving me hell. . .'

She knelt to take off his shoes. He caught her hand as she straightened up. 'You have to get your trousers off,' she told him gently, withdrawing it.

He shouted with laughter at the naïve remark. 'What an invitation! Now why didn't I think of that?' he murmured, shaking his head.

'You know exactly what I meant,' she told him severely, aware that another crisis was approaching. 'You do that yourself. Then I'll come and have a look at your leg.'

Handing him his towelling robe, she made for the door.

When she returned a few minutes later he was sitting on the bed where she had left him, both legs bare, waiting for her. 'So,' he asked, 'what do you think?' He stretched his worst leg out to her probing fingers, wincing when she touched the trouble-spots.

'I expect it's some strain and a little nerve pressure,' she explained as she began to massage the tautened muscles gently, kneading into them as she had been taught. 'It's still early days, Mike; you expect too much of yourself—too soon.'

'I shall miss you, Sarah. . .' burst from him as, with a quick movement, he held her shoulders, drawing her towards him so that she couldn't get up. His bare knees gripped her waist and even as her hands pressed against his bare chest, the soft vibrant hair under her fingers, she knew that this simply could not go on.

Suddenly he let her go. She got to her feet, saw him tremble and knot his towelling robe. Then he put his head in his hands.

'Get into bed, Mike. You've had quite a day. I have, too. See you in the morning. Goodnight.'

'Goodnight, Sarah,' he muttered, his voice husky, meeting her eyes at last, 'or is it "Goodbye"?'

After a time she knew she was not going to sleep. She got up, going to stand at the mesh-covered window. Moonlight over the prairies: the title for a song, she mused, her emotions still confused.

CHAPTER ELEVEN

SARAH's thoughts were chaotic as she slipped into bed. Her nerves were stretched and taut. Too much had happened emotionally in these last short months. Much too much, and now her pent-up feelings were released in a flood of silent tears. All she wanted, needed desperately, was to be really loved, deeply, and to give her own love in return.

She got up and stood by the window, calmer now, looking out at the moonlit prairies and distant hills.

Tomorrow she would be leaving here and driving back to Vancouver with Neil. If only she knew how he really felt about her. Had she read too much into his sometimes tender approach? More than he had meant her to? Or perhaps she had hidden her own feelings too much. Perhaps he was uncertain about her state of mind concerning him. Maybe, now that she had achieved what she set out to do—help restore Mike to some of his former image and strength so that he could at least face the future with confidence—it was time to go back to where she belonged. A new life, in another hospital, in another part of England, and perhaps some time, somewhere she would find happiness. Right now it was evading her at every turn of the road. Oh, Neil; tomorrow I have to know, she thought miserably. I can't go on this way.

Dawn came early, a lovely pink glow in the sky, spreading to meet the sun at the start of another summer day.

She heard Mike go along the corridor while she was in the shower, and when she went out to the veranda he was already there.

'You're early,' she said, assessing his face, heavy-eyed like her own.

'Mmm. I got up to watch the dawn. It's usually my time of day. Shall we have breakfast?'

His eyes met hers briefly and, she knew, deliberately, before indicating a small gift-wrapped box on the table.

'Just something to show my appreciation,' he murmured. 'Midge told me it's the one you use.'

She unwrapped the small box while he watched her face, to find her favourite perfume.

'Oh—thank you.' She wanted to cry. 'It was—very thoughtful of you.'

'It's I who should be grateful,' he said solemnly, noticing that she was looking down the driveway to where Joe and another cowhand were galloping their horses, and wrongly interpreting it to mean that she couldn't wait to see her surgeon appear to take her away with him.

Neil phoned halfway through the morning to say that he was on his way. They were sitting on the veranda, drinking coffee, when the Cougar's long nose appeared and sped up to the house. Mike was watching Sarah and saw the slow flush creep into her cheeks as she stood up, waiting while Neil got out, slammed the car door and came to the veranda steps. Casually dressed but groomed as always, he made an immediate impact. His dark eyes scanned them both before saying lightly, 'Hi—you look great. Every inch a rancher, Mike. Didn't realise you were so tall. How are the legs?'

'Fine,' Mike answered. 'Would you like some coffee? Or a drink?' He was the host.

'Coffee, please.'

'I'll make some more,' Sarah said, conscious that both men watched her while she picked up the tray.

As she left them alone she heard them talking, and she hoped that Neil would be satisfied with his patient's progress and that she hadn't made too hasty a decision to leave now. She felt fairly confident and that it was probably just a question of time. Besides which his physio would monitor him almost daily and would soon get in touch with the hospital if there was any reason to do so.

She longed to be alone with Neil. He would want to know what had led up to her sudden decision to come back to Vancouver now, just at this time.

Carefully filling the coffee-pot and placing it on a tray with mugs, milk and brown cane sugar, she carried it out to the two men on the veranda and began to pour. They stopped talking as she did so and she wondered just what they had been discussing. Surely, not herself?

Lunch was almost a charade. Mike seemed to treat her with a possessiveness which embarrassed her, while Neil also tried to give the impression that he and Sarah were closer than they were. It was she who played it down and put the whole thing in perspective once more.

After lunch Mike led the way to the stables, anxious to show off his horses and the new foal. He managed quite well with only one stick, while Sarah reminded him that he should be using two. He changed the subject by pointing towards the hills on the boundary of his land and suggesting that Sarah should take Neil and show him the ranges and cattle, stretching away to the foothills, the boundaries of his ranch.

Then he turned to make it back to the house with difficulty. And Sarah wouldn't be there to see that he rested, because Neil had said that he wanted to leave fairly soon, and again she looked serious.

But there was happiness too, as she, with Neil beside her, walked through a field of clover and yellow wild flowers and she pointed out some pink Indian Paintbrush growing in the tall grass. Her hair blew across her face in the soft breezes, and happiness shone from her eyes in her now more abandoned mood because Neil was here beside her, breathing in the soft sweet-smelling pine air of the prairies, and she was going back with him. It was over now, the ordeal she had set herself: Mike was restored to his former male image. Well—almost. But soon he might not need sticks and then slowly he could try out his horses, and anything else he chose to do.

Like her, Neil had also unwound now that they were away from the ranch house, entering into her mood, taking deep breaths, laughing at her futile attempts to keep the errant breezes from blowing her hair in all directions.

'So,' he laughed, 'you are almost a native now. It's done you good, this break up here, away from—things, hasn't it? Mike isn't too happy about letting you leave, I guess. Was it your decision, or his?'

'Mine,' she answered truthfully. 'It's time to get back to the hospital and Midge will look after his more material needs—and the physio and hospital between them will take care of him physically.'

'What about the girlfriend? Isn't she around?'

'Yes.'

She told him about last night's meal at the Boat-house. Neil made no comment. But back at the house he had just stowed her bags away in the boot when Monique's red car came speeding up the drive towards them.

Sarah turned to Mike, her eyes meeting his. 'Good-bye,' she murmured. 'Please—take care.'

'Monique. . .' His face tensed suddenly.

'Weren't you expecting her to come?'

'No. . .'

'Perhaps it's because she knows I'm leaving today.'

'I'm sure it is,' he said tersely. The car door slammed and Monique came quickly towards them, her hand held out to Neil before she reached him.

'Hi. You just have to be Dr Patterson, don't you? I guess we owe Mike's recovery to you.' She gave him a scintillating smile which Neil returned.

'Not entirely my doing,' he told her. 'These two people here have been working very hard at it.'

I wonder how she does it? Sarah thought as she saw that Neil was getting the full treatment, until Mike came limping over to her again and she saw that Monique had broken off and was watching him.

'Goodbye, Sarah,' he said quietly. 'Thank you for—everything.' His hand covered hers tightly. 'I won't forget what you've done for me—all your patience.'

'Goodbye, Mike. Keep up your exercises, and if you have any problems call us any time.'

'Sure.' Then, turning to Neil he said, 'I guess I have a lot to thank you for too, Doc. Putting me back together again. . .'

'You've made it, Mike. That's the important thing. Take it easy; you can't rush these things. But in any case I'll be seeing you in Outpatients some time. As Sarah says, we're there if you have any problems. OK, then—we'll be off now.' Both he and Sarah smiled at Monique and left.

As the car gathered speed Sarah turned to wave; Monique was still standing at Mike's side, so it had to be all right again between them. She wanted to think of them together again. Somehow it put the whole situation into perspective. Neil heard her sigh of relief as she moved closer against his shoulder. He had obviously been thinking about them too because he commented drily, 'Mike's girlfriend is rather dynamic, isn't she?'

Sarah smiled. 'You could say that. Something of a challenge to him now, I think, which isn't a bad thing. He needs her around to have the drive to get back into his lifestyle again.'

He threw her a quick glance before turning on to the main highway. 'Wasn't your decision to come back with me made rather suddenly, Sarah?'

She had been expecting him to ask this. 'Yes. Yes, it

was. But I'm sure it was the right decision. Should I
have discussed it with you first?'

'Not necessarily. You were better able to assess him,
being here with him continually. I think he can manage
perfectly well if he doesn't try to rush things. It's an
appropriate time, actually. But I am amazed at his
progress. The end result is extremely gratifying.
Thanks to you, I'd say. It—can't always have been
easy.'

'There were a few problems,' she said lightly, 'but
we overcame those as they arose. He had a great deal
of readjusting to do. At least it was worth it.'

'Good. And now I have you all to myself for the
next few hours.'

Sarah sat quietly beside him, absorbing the scenery
as the car covered the kilometres, revelling in the
freedom of no longer feeling responsible for her
patient's welfare.

She sat with Neil's shoulder against hers and her arm
along the window edge, the roof being down. Casting
surreptitious glances at his profile concentrated on the
busy highway, at the way his hair grew and was shaped
into his neck, at his hands, those long capable fingers
on the wheel, she wondered what his thoughts were
where she was concerned.

'By the way,' Neil said suddenly, breaking into her
musings. 'Charles and Andrea want us to go over for a
meal some time. I think she'll contact you. OK?'

'Yes. I'd like that.' Sarah switched back to the
present moment and the length of motorway stretching
ahead interminably. Neil had already done this once
today already. 'You must have left very early this
morning,' she reflected, glancing at him.

'Very,' he said, giving her a brief glance. In that split
second their eyes met. It was enough to send a shaft of
excitement through every part of her body so that she
kept her eyes firmly on the road after that. Heavens—
what on earth was she going to do about this? True—

she hadn't seen him for almost a month, but she must not let him see what just one glance could do to her.

His feelings were under wraps. She had no way of knowing that he was having great difficulty in keeping them there. But it was exhilarating just the same as she listened to some of the social dates which would be coming during the next months. 'And there are two lectures I thought you might like to come to with me, mainly dealing with trauma in orthopaedics. I know you've done all that for State Registration in the UK, but I think you might like a new approach, from the nursing angle.'

'Oh, yes,' she said eagerly. 'When is this?'

'I'll check on the dates.'

'Fine.'

He went on, 'And I must try to take you across to Victoria before the summer disappears.' He saw the corners of her mouth lift as the invitations caught on. She had seemed a little out of reach today and he wondered why.

Now she discovered that the injection of new ideas was acting like a tonic. Something to look forward to. Neil wanted her with him. It was balm to her bruised ego. His concern for her and obvious pleasure in being with her was healing the bruised emotions deep in her heart. The upsurges and downbeats in the past few weeks had not been conducive to personal clear thinking—not to mention the initial shocks she had already suffered prior to that time.

'Vancouver—five kilometres,' she read aloud after the seemingly endless driving was almost over.

'You're tired.'

'Yes—I think I am. So must you be. . .'

The highways were crowded as they came nearer to the city, and Neil had to concentrate even more as they entered the suburbs. The mountains which Sarah had seen in the distance—in fact, the whole coastal range—rose up like sentinels. Snow-tipped, even while the sun eased away the ice-cappings, they still glittered like thousands of diamond chips in the evening glow which covered the more modern buildings in the immediate vicinity.

'I think the whole of BC is out on a leisure weekend,' Neil observed drily as they reached the outskirts. 'I had intended taking you for a meal out this evening, but I'm having second thoughts. It could be a bit crowded everywhere and I haven't booked.' He glanced at her quickly as he drove through the main street. 'What about coming back to my place? I'm sure I can rustle up something, if it's only a chicken salad. There's cheese, and my cupboards are quite well-stocked. It would be far less tiring.'

He waited, not looking at her now. 'I'd love to come,' she told him, her eyes dancing because she had sensed that he had given it a lot of thought before asking her, and there was just a trace of uncertainty in his voice. 'I—mustn't be too late because I need to get ready for the morning.'

'That's OK, then.' He swung the car into a side-street and headed for the suburbs. 'Be there in ten minutes.'

Sarah waited impatiently to see his house, and soon he turned from the tree-lined avenue into the gateway of a typical Canadian house of wood and brick. She loved it at once. The golden evening sun slashed the front windows; there was a tree in bloom on the front lawn and flowers in the borders.

'It's beautiful,' she murmured, leaning forward.

'You like it?'

'Oh, yes. . .'

'So do I, and I'm glad I decided to buy it when I did because it's increased in price quite a bit. I didn't feel too happy in an apartment.'

'Do you garden?'

'Not more than I can help. No—I've a guy who

comes in a couple of times a week and keeps it going for me.'

Six steps led up to the front door, which was wooden, and a secondary mesh door to keep out the mosquitos.

Inside, a flight of stairs led to the basement, comprising another bathroom, a games and exercise room and the utilities.

'The other rooms are on this floor,' he said, leading Sarah towards a large kitchen at the back. 'The lounge is over there; here is my study-cum-library, or whatever. And there are two bedrooms and a bath and shower-room. Now—you have it all. Would you like a drink or supper, or both?'

She followed him into the pine kitchen which had a round table and four chairs and lots of work room. There were brown and white striped curtains at the windows and a door leading to a veranda at the back, and right away he made for the fridge, which was enormous by Sarah's standards.

'Shall we start on the supper?' she suggested while he was already putting two glasses on the table and producing wine from the fridge, proceeding to pour them each an almost full glass.

'Are you hungry?' He was enjoying this.

'Yes. Are you?'

'Andrea gave me some of her delicious cream of lettuce soup. She makes it herself. Do you prefer it hot or cold?'

'Cold, I think, please.'

Next came the chicken and salad, and then a black-currant pie was popped into the oven to heat while they ate.

'No cream, I'm afraid; I'm careful cholesterol-wise, but we could compromise with low-fat ice-cream.'

'It's wonderful,' she said happily, and meant it. 'I had no idea you were so domesticated.'

'Ah—not everyone does.' He grinned. 'You are very privileged.'

'I'm glad,' she said simply.

The look he gave her then caused more tremors along her nerve-ends and she was no longer able to meet his eyes. He mustn't know what he was doing to her. Even just being here with him in his home was exciting enough. And he was so different today from his hospital image. Today she was very aware of his masculine image: his natural one, which was usually covered by a dark suit or white coat, was really there all the time. She closed her eyes against her trailing thoughts, realising that he had been watching her and was reaching for her fingers lying in her lap.

'Let's take our coffee outside,' he suggested, not quite certain of what he thought he was seeing in her downcast look. Together they went out on to the veranda which ran across the back of the house. Everything was beginning to be dream-like to Sarah, an impression fortunately revealed only to herself. There was no way he could know about the rush of longing which had hit her a moment ago. She drew a very deep breath as they sat together on a rustic seat watching the sun go down in a blaze of orange and flame-streaked glory.

'Everything here seems that much more spectacular,' she mused. 'We have lovely sunsets in Dorset, but this seems awe-inspiring, and I'm beginning to wonder why I'm still here. I suppose it's decision time, now that I've done what I set out to do.' She turned to look at him. 'It's really why I decided to stay, isn't it?'

'Is—that the only reason?' he asked softly.

She turned to meet his eyes, her resolve shaken by something in his voice.

'Sarah—I. . .'

She waited because his facial muscles had suddenly tensed and, pulling her to her feet, his hands slid up her arms to her shoulders and she was suddenly close to his lithe body, aware of him now as never before. There was an urgency in his kiss, his mouth warm on

hers, his arms tightening and his heart pounding against
her thin blouse; then, without her realising it, Sarah's
arms were around his neck, her body close to his, and
she was kissing him back, their kisses deep and creating
a breathlessness in both until they needed air and their
flushed faces were pressed together.

'Oh, Sarah—what am I going to do about you? I—
want to make love to you. . .desperately.'

Her head moved against the curve of his shoulder.
Her fingers slipped inside the cotton covering his chest.
'I know. . .' she said softly.

She wanted to tell him that she wanted him to make
love to her, but something held her back. And now he
was gently putting her from him.

'I—guess I got carried away; sorry about that,' he
muttered. 'I'm going to take you back to your apartment now. We can both do with an early night after
today's long drive and I know we have a heavy work
load tomorrow.'

You are making excuses, she thought as she went
with him to the door. His kisses, his body, so close to
hers, had left her feeling devastated. She wanted to
cry, biting her lips to keep them from trembling. How
could he draw back, switch off so deliberately? What
was he afraid of? What was the reason behind it?
Perhaps he was reluctant to get into a deeper relationship; perhaps he thought she couldn't handle merging
a personal one with their professional life yet. He was
fully aware of her response to him tonight. Or did he
think she went around revealing her heart to any man
who kissed her? Of course not. She was being imma-
ture now. There were no answers, just a feeling of
disappointment and an insecurity in their relations from
now on.

She guessed from Neil's set profile as he turned into
the street where the apartments were that he was
annoyed about his own momentary loss of control.

He stopped the car and, taking her bags from his

boot, carried them into the block and through to her door.

'Aren't you coming in?' She looked up at him, her eyes eloquent.

He couldn't stand any more, simply shaking his head and squeezing her fingers, then turned to go, saying 'Goodnight, Sarah,' in a voice totally unlike his normal one.

Slipping her key in the lock, she looked back along the corridor but he had already gone.

Neil, driving back to his own house, was emotionally off-key. Rarely did he allow his feelings to become out of control. He was an even-tempered man, rarely letting annoyance become more than that, but tonight he had realised the depth of his feelings for Sarah and become blinded to everything but his desperate need to love her. Also her immediate responsiveness, her eagerness for his kisses had shaken him to a new realisation that she was a woman in every way and no longer wanted or needed his protectiveness. She wanted him as a man. There had been no need to hold back. So why had he? Couldn't he trust himself? Or Sarah? Was it because of Rachel? Or because of Sarah's words about it being decision time? About returning to England. Well—he was going to have to do something about that, wasn't he? Something positive. It was just a question of when or where, because he really loved that girl. But hadn't he known that, right from the start? From the moment she had walked towards him across the corridor in Intensive Care. The apprehensive look in those eyes which had sought and found his even then, waiting for what he had had to tell her, responding bravely. Yes—that was the moment, if he was truthful.

And Sarah, lying in bed after putting everything ready for the morning, was also going over their day and the evening which had followed. His rising passion and her own. What did he want from her? Or she from him?

He had been so protective towards her. What was now in his mind? Or her own? What did she really want from him? Even an egotistical primitive urge from him to finally become her lover? Did she want that from him? It wasn't that—of course it wasn't. He was too nice. Had given her back a reason, a way to go forward again after her world had overturned a few months before. Was it any wonder that she had grasped at having another caring relationship, like straws on a sea of uncertainty? So maybe she was reading too much into it. In her heart was a sliver of doubt, because he did not reveal all of himself. So why should he? It was a part of his arrogance and, she had to admit, also his appeal.

Unanswered questions were not conducive to a good night's sleep. Too many memories came crowding in until Sarah read for a while in desperation to free her mind from what had actually led up to that time. But in the very early hours she slept deeply, until her alarm bell woke her to face whatever lay ahead for the coming day.

No one would have guessed at her wretched night when she walked through the corridors on her way to her wards, looking cool and fresh in her white uniform, her head high. Here among other nurses, interns and doctors, the equipment and trolleys, smells and sounds of the antiseptic atmosphere, her mind returned to disciplined thinking and doing, and everything else was dismissed.

Her patients comfortable, she took an early coffee-break, sitting next to Debby who was obviously pleased that she was back, and full of curiosity about Mike's progress and, more subtly, her own.

'How did you get back yesterday? You ought to get yourself some wheels, Sarah.'

'Dr Patterson drove me back.'

'Gee. In that sports car? Lucky you. What was he like? I mean, did he talk to you? All that way, sitting beside him. . .'

'Of course he did,' Sarah told her with an amused smile. 'He's very nice. . .'

'Oh, sure. But he can be off-putting sometimes. But how is Mike Rayner? And what about the girlfriend? Oh, come on—I want to hear it all. . .'

'I can't now,' Sarah said, finishing her coffee. 'I shouldn't have come down anyway but I really needed that coffee.'

Neil was going through the corridor when she came out of the lift.

'Good morning, Nurse,' he said for the benefit of two interns coming towards them. 'I'm just coming to see my patients. Is all well?'

He gave her a searching look when she answered quietly, professionally and didn't smile. 'Good morning, Dr Patterson,' she said, and went into room six without looking at him again. But she wondered what he would have said if the two interns had not been approaching.

When she answered the phone in the early afternoon, Neil asked, 'Nurse Hillier?'

'Yes.'

'Dr Patterson here. Sarah, I'll pick you up in the car park around six-thirty. OK?'

'Yes. Thank you.' Her voice had involuntarily softened.

When Sarah left the building that evening the sky was rapidly darkening as a storm swept in over the mountains, and she slid into his car seat, a grateful smile lighting up her face. 'Thanks. It was a nice thought.'

He threw her a keen look, more speculative than curious. 'You're in need of an uplift, Nurse Hillier.'

'Maybe.'

'Are you—going out tonight?'

'Not tonight.'

The car stopped outside her apartment and he leaned across to open her door, his French aftershave reminding her again of being held so close in his arms on Sunday evening. But before he could speak she had already opened it and got out quickly.

His face was serious as he looked up at her through the window, rain-spattered now.

'Goodnight, Sarah.'

'Goodnight.'

He took off at once and she went into the building, dodging the puddles rapidly forming on the asphalt.

The room seemed hot and airless until she threw up the windows, all covered with fine mesh. Then she opened a letter from Sister Maine which had been lying on her doormat.

With a mug of coffee in her hand she sat down to read it. Afterwards, when nostalgia had passed, she gave serious thought to going back to England. Could she bear to leave Neil? Could she simply turn her back and fly out across the ice-floes, the vast expanse of sea—back to Dorset which would always be home? For the first time she really loved a man with whom she could spend the rest of her life. She only wanted to be where he was. If only he felt the same way. She would never forget his support, like a hand held out to her when she had needed it so desperately. While she was in the vortex of shock after her father's accident, Neil had kept her thinking and doing, even as far as helping the other victim of that serious accident, so that her emotions were transferred to working for his survival. But that was over now and she could cope on her own. Except that she had fallen in love.

Her feeling of restlessness grew. Outside the streets were steaming in the warmth of the evening sun as the summer storm moved away. She decided to go out in the fresher air. A walk—that was what she needed.

Changing quickly into a pale green linen two-piece,

her bag over her shoulder, she left the building. The janitor watched her go, wondering why she hadn't a car, the only tenant who didn't.

Sarah decided to walk around the block, past the department store where she could window-shop and through a park. Somehow she took a wrong turning and walked much further than she had intended, finding herself in the downtown area, but only feeling really frightened when she came to a dead end with the stench of rubbish and curry smells wafting out from steaming kitchens. She knew she was lost. How had she got here?

Turning back, she saw the loitering figures of three shabby youths emerging from an alley and coming slowly towards her. She began to run, turning into another narrow alley, aware that they were following. She was panicking now, dashing blindly between two buildings and coming out into a quiet street. A car was disappearing from view, but another, zooming around a corner, suddenly slowed down behind her. 'Oh, no—I'm not a pick-up,' she ground out. But there was absolutely no one else on the pavement and another car simply drove by. She started to run again. Then she heard her name.

'Sarah—wait. . .'

Only one person said her name like that. She looked over her shoulder. Neil was already leaning across to open the door for her. He looked very angry.

'What the hell are you doing?' he asked, his eyes glaring at her.

She was still trembling, breathless and almost in tears. 'Things just don't happen this way!' she whispered disbelievingly.

He began to drive slowly round the block. 'You're out of bounds. Why on earth are you wandering around alone in this downtown area? Surely you're not that naïve? You must be mad. Drop-outs, addicts, drug

pedlars—this is where they hang out. It's compara-
tively early yet, but later. . . You've seen it all before
at the hospital—in Casualty.'

'I'm not on Casualty,' she said stubbornly.

'You soon might have been. Why take risks? You
said you weren't going out tonight.'

'Oh—don't go on about it. . .' She was near to tears.
He turned the car round.

'It was a hundred-to-one chance I came by.'

There was less anger in his tone now and she asked
quietly, 'Why did you?'

'I've come from my appointment with a patient.
Rather a sad case. I'll tell you about it some time. I'm
going to have her in next week and she'll be one of our
special patients, I think. That is, if you are still going
to be here.'

'Of course I'll be here. . .' she began, then remembered that she had told him she hadn't yet decided.

The car stopped in front of a Chinese restaurant.
'Would you like to have a meal with me? I haven't
eaten yet.'

She nodded gratefully, wondering how he knew that
she had come out without eating too.

They didn't speak again until they were inside and
being greeted by a very pretty Chinese girl wearing
national costume. Seated on cushioned chairs, they
waited for the wine Neil had ordered. Sarah sat quite
still, a little overawed, but thrilled by the atmosphere,
the music in the background like tinkling bells trilling
somewhere above them. She sat quite still, her head a
little back, with all her natural poise. How proud he
was of her and how lovely she looked tonight.

He was still looking at her thoughtfully when their
wine was poured. She caught his expression and smiled
as he lifted his glass.

'You're looking at me as you do at one of your
patients when you're not sure about them or their
symptoms,' she said tentatively.

'I'm not sure—about *you*, Sarah. I think we have to be honest with each other, don't you? It's time for that now.'

She met his eyes, hesitating only a little. 'Yes. I think so too. We know so little about each other.'

'Some things—not others. Probably because we happen to be inwardly private people.' He shrugged, 'But then, that's part of our make-up—isn't it?'

She didn't answer as their meal began to arrive, all the small, interesting dishes which were an essential part of it, both knowing that what they most wanted to say to each other must wait until they were alone.

CHAPTER TWELVE

SARAH and Neil left immediately after the meal was over, he having some notes to go through when he reached home.

'And we both have a long day tomorrow,' he said as they walked out to the parked car. 'Oh—I almost forgot, Andrea called this evening before I left. They're having a small party on Saturday and would like us both to go for dinner. I think it has to be some kind of celebration but I'll try to find out more. Are you free?'

'Yes. I'll look forward to it. Are you?'

'Oh, yes.' They were, she realised, being very careful but, before she left the car, he took her face in both hands, kissing her gently.

'Goodnight, Sarah.'

'Goodnight, Neil.' Her voice sounded normal but her eyes were starry.

Next day was, as he had predicted, a long one, but passing quickly because she was charge nurse for that day and the next. Nursing on an orthopaedic ward was rather different from that on a general or surgical ward. Great skill was needed when a patient had to be lifted or moved. A lot of investigations were routine, but many were not and the nurse in charge had to take responsibility in relation to these.

Sarah had long ago gone through her training on the locomotor system and was now carefully teaching the two juniors who had joined the team, also informing them of the extra care needed when limbs were splinted, over soreness and careful drying. All these things were part of a nurse's day-to-day work and Sarah knew how angry Neil or any of the surgeons would be if soreness were discovered anywhere. There were drugs to be given and notes of the resultant observations kept. Also nursing had its psychological factors: which were what Sarah had had to deal with in Mike Rayner's case. Both patients and their relatives were, in this hospital, kept aware of their progress and told why, in some cases, certain positions had to be maintained to assist their recovery.

Neil was very good at doing that, and Sarah, together with the rest of his little knot of medics and two registrars, stood listening to him today, as he explained, 'This patient has an acute exacerbation of rheumatical arthritis. She is not only in a great deal of pain, but because it is, as you know, an infection of the bone—in this case the joints of her hands, together with the wrists—Mrs Kelso is feeling quite ill in herself and is no longer able to maintain her own independence. We shall administer anti-inflammatory drugs and analgesia, and Mrs Kelso's wrists will be splinted. Nurse—perhaps you will explain to her why splintage is necessary. Rest, of course, too. Don't worry, Mrs Kelso; we'll soon have you feeling quite a lot better.'

They moved on, and Sarah, making her own notes, was enjoying the involvement. They were working together as a team for the first time, she felt, she and Neil. Here on the wards, in front of the others, it was all very professional.

Next door, Ray Fielding, in his late twenties, the son of a wealthy rancher, was recovering from a meniscectomy and needed static quadriceps exercise for a few minutes each hour. His knee had a dressing with a pressure bandage and had to be kept on a pillow. Here the nurse in charge kept careful watch on his circulation. He was sitting up, and Neil was obviously very pleased with his progress—as he was with his other patients, and at the end of the day went off feeling quite satisfied with his day's work.

The only real niggle was Sarah. But he thought that even with her there had to be a way to achieve his desire. For he was as lovesick as an adolescent. He began to make plans of his own.

When he phoned in the evening she heard that more intimate note in his voice. He seemed in high spirits too and said that he was really looking forward to Saturday evening. Because he had something to ask her. Something important to them both.

'Does it have to wait until then?'

'Yes. I think so. I'm not completely sure of your reaction. So, yes. We'll talk on Saturday. I'll pick you up, of course.'

So she would just have to wait.

Friday was Neil's day in theatre and there was very little chance to say anything to each other. It was a very tiring day for the surgeons, and fraught with decisions and traumas. So Sarah did her job, looking after all her patients as expected, and was on duty part of Saturday too, when Neil didn't come in unless he was needed urgently.

But he was there promptly at seven, coming into her small hall and taking her at once into his arms but releasing her, standing back to comment on the way she looked. Tonight she wore earrings. 'I haven't seen you like this before. Black really suits you, doesn't it? Oh, Sarah, I'm so proud of you. You are a lovely woman.'

'Thanks. I thought I should rise to the occasion. Should we take them something if it's a celebration? I've bought some flowers for Andrea.'

'I've got some malt whisky in the car and a flower arrangement for her too. We'll discover the rest when we arrive.'

'Have you noticed. . .' she spoke thoughtfully as they went out to the car '. . .that they always invite us together?'

'I wonder why?' he teased, holding her arm as he walked beside her, wearing his dark suit this evening.

The closeness they had found at the Chinese restaurant was still there tonight. She was content, knowing that whatever he was going to ask her had to be when he decided was the right time.

It was a lovely party, the atmosphere perfect, the guests chosen carefully from the medical world and some of Andrea's own friends. Neil and Sarah seemed very important for some reason, and Andrea's eyes were all-seeing when they came in together and Neil guided her protectively among the other guests. Andrea knew at once that something between them was different—had been resolved—and she was longing to confide her instincts to her husband.

It was the Sutcliffes' silver wedding anniversary. They purposely hadn't told anyone, not wanting the usual flow of presents to arrive with their guests—'Just to celebrate with you, our special friends,' Charles told them as they sat around the huge dining-table shining with silver settings and glass and a beautiful flower arrangement in the centre. And as everyone drank to Charles and Andrea, Sarah's eyes went to Neil's and what she saw there set her own heart beating much too fast. Just one look could do that to her! She found herself looking down and away from him while she took a few deep breaths.

But he saw the light in her eyes and the deep breaths and he knew that the time was right. Tonight—he would ask her.

When the dusk was shading the garden where lanterns and small coloured lights were coming on, Neil took her to the furthest part where shrubs and trees hid them from view but from where they could glimpse the sea. With his arm around her, he said, 'Sarah—I want you to come away with me next weekend. Will you?'

He heard her small gasp of surprise.

'Please listen: I want to show you a very special place. You may think this strange—it's a kind of secret place, where I go sometimes to recover when things become too pressured. OK, it's my hide-away if you like. No one else knows about it. Only you now. It's a simple wooden chalet beside a lake, quite deep in the woods and surrounded by tall spruce firs. And the peace is indescribable. Nothing but the whispering branches and the birds. Oh—sometimes, a few chipmunks looking for nuts. I do want to take you there, so much. I'm driving up there next weekend. Please come with me. It's very important, for us both.'

Her eyes were wide and searching as they looked deeply into his. He still held both her hands in his, waiting for her answer. After a moment he looked away, squaring his shoulders.

'I shouldn't have asked you,' he said huskily. 'You only have to say no, Sarah.'

'But, I want to come with you. More than anything else,' she confessed, just for once listening to the dictates of her heart, her eyes raised to his.

'Oh, my darling. . .' He kissed her passionately, and again, as if he couldn't believe what he was hearing.

And it was Andrea who noticed that they came in from the garden, Sarah with her hand in Neil's and that special glow which belonged only to those in love. But they didn't say anything, except to have a quiet few minutes together after the others had all gone. Their hosts wanted to know how Sarah had settled in her apartment, about Mike up at the ranch and how she was slowly becoming accustomed to living in Vancouver.

'I'm on duty tomorrow,' she said, when Neil suggested they should go. 'My Sunday duty.'

But next weekend, she told herself, I am not. Instead, I am going to be with Neil the whole weekend. It was a disturbing and yet exciting thought.

Being an extra busy week, it flew by, but at last duties were handed over and other nurses delegated for her weekend off. On Friday morning Sarah's case was in the boot of the Cougar beside Neil's and already he was closing the door on her in the white bucket seat. They were off. Both were dressed casually in cool tops and linen trousers, and when they stopped for coffee he rolled back the top of the car and now the soft wind caught at her hair. His too. The surgeon had definitely been left behind this morning, which was a lovely sunny one—with a sky startlingly blue against the few soft white clouds drifting harmlessly over the mountains.

His car was built for speed and for most of the way he drove in the fast lane. He didn't talk much. There was no need. She was quite happy to just sit beside him. This was today a form of escapism. His thoughts were his own. At last this girl who had taken up a great deal of his private thinking-time recently was here beside him. Until now any permanent relationship would have been a little out of context. Sarah? He found her quite irresistible. If anyone could make him change his mind, it was she. Hadn't she already done so?

He stopped the car to let her see the rushing Fraser River, cascading and roaring through the canyons far below. 'At this place gold rush miners were murdered by Indians watching from the hills,' he told her.

'I've read about them,' she said as she watched the angry waters. 'I did quite a lot of it at the ranch. Mike had some very good books on the pioneer days too.'

'We would need much more time than a weekend for you to see half of the phenomena in the Rocky Mountains,' he said as they got back into the car and were soon speeding again. 'The Columbia Icefields, for one. Athabasca Falls—probably the highest and noisiest you'll ever see. Banff, with fantastic scenery. It's another world.'

'I've never seen so many mountains, nor so strong a river—it's foaming down there. And how close the railway is! Only inches away. It looks dangerous.'

'I guess it does. But that train takes you three

thousand miles across Canada and it's so scenic they have an glass observation coach on top.'

Later he showed her where the Thompson joined the Fraser. 'Marvellous for salmon and blue trout. I fished here for a week in the spring. Just before you came. In fact, we'll make a stop if you like. They have excellent coffee at the chalet.'

It was good to stretch her legs, though, he reminded her, they were not even halfway yet.

In the early afternoon the mountains began to take over the scene. Sarah couldn't absorb the distances of vast and endless motorways and, at last, the Yellowhead Pass and, through the shrouds of misty clouds high above them, the towering peaks and ridges of a gigantic mountain with snow on the summit and on the outer purple slopes. It was in front of them.

'That,' Neil told her, 'is Mount Robson. Awesome, isn't it? Highest peak in the Rockies. In winter it looks like a giant iceberg.'

'How high do you suppose it is?' Sarah was spellbound.

'Nearly thirteen thousand feet, I guess. The whole range constitutes the Rockies. Five hundred miles of them. We're three thousand feet above sea-level ourselves now. Did you realise that?'

'No wonder the air is so pure. It's a bit heady, isn't it? You didn't warn me that it would be this spectacular, Neil.'

Later still they left the road through the woods and took another, little more than a track, leading to the cabin, as he called it, but the wooden veranda had to make it a chalet.

Inside, which smelled of pine, a log fire was laid ready. The wood floors were covered with thick rugs. There was a chesterfield drawn up in front of the fire, low tables and other armchairs. The cabin had been built of wood and lined inside with wood. The windows were small but hung with brightly coloured Indian

patterned material. And in the bedroom Sarah saw
that the divan was covered with an Indian cover to
match.

Lamps hung from the rafters. A very small kitchen
was simply furnished with a cupboard, china and
cooking pans.

'Primitive, I know,' Neil said happily, coming up
behind her and nuzzling her neck. 'But I usually quite
enjoy it.'

He had brought an ice-box with him and champagne
too. Sarah watched delightedly as he plunged it into
the cold stream just outside the door. Then he lit the
fire because it was colder under the trees and a little
damp too.

Later Sarah laid their meal on a rough-hewn table in
front of it, while he unpacked the salads. He had even
remembered crusty rolls and cheeses. Fruit too. Everything they might need.

'You really are a most unpredictable man, aren't
you?' she murmured, enjoying every moment, barely
able to take in everything that was happening to them,
finding it difficult to tie up this man—deftly slicing
tomatoes and peppers and wearing brown boots and a
sweater now over his jeans—with the image of Dr
Patterson in his perfectly cut suits and beautiful shirts.
This man had a wood-ash smear on his chin, and his
hands were not at all the surgeon's hands she knew.

When the meal was over, the plates washed and put
away, and the smell of coffee pervading the cabin and
the quiet darkness of the forest all around, they both
sat on the long chesterfield: he at one end and she at
the other. He had wanted for so long to share this
cabin with Sarah and now he just wanted to watch her.
He didn't think he could ever tire of the changing
expressions of her face. Over the rim of her glass Sarah
watched the dancing flames bursting into a crescendo
of yellow and orange sparks. Her lips curved dreamily
and Neil, with a half-smile on his face which she only

saw when she turned to look at him, put down his glass and moved towards her.

But her arms were already reaching for him, her mouth waiting hungrily for his. When she was weak with his kisses, roused in a way she had never been before to a deep, pulsating need, almost overwhelmed by her own untapped passion, he was at last admitting that he loved her.

The words burst from him as he pressed his lips to her throat. 'Oh, God—I do love you, Sarah. I've never wanted any woman as I want you. To be with you—is heaven. Believe it, my darling.'

'Oh, Neil—what took you so long?' she asked shamelessly.

He pushed the hair from her eyes as she leaned away from him, his hands gentle on her face, her eyes—her lips. 'Because, my darling, of your naturally emotional state of mind after your father. You looked towards me because I was the first person involved. And then there was Mike. You needed him too. In some way he also helped you get over your father's death. I wasn't really sure how you felt about him. I thought he was getting serious about you. And who could blame him? So—I just had to wait, and to be sure I could rearrange my own life. You see, I've avoided a permanent relationship—until now. But, darling, I can't envisage any future without you. I want to share every day, every night with you. For the rest of my life.'

'And I you. . .' she whispered, her words lost in the pressure of his lips on her face and her neck, his enveloping arms crushing her body and a now-demanding passion unleashed at last.

And now there was no wish to go back as Sarah was swept along with him, and outside the wind moaned among the tall pines and the logs died away to smouldering embers.

And in the morning the embers were rekindled, because outside in the forest a soft summer rain was falling and they wandered, hand in hand, beneath the dripping trees, sharing a happiness too great for words.

Sarah knew she would always remember the scent of the aspens and the pine needles beneath their feet.

They would come here again, just the two of them, and perhaps later with their children, and each time their love would be renewed and they would always remember this first time.

Mills & Boon

APRIL 1991 HARDBACK TITLES

ROMANCE

Passionate Betrayal *Jacqueline Baird*	3476	0 263 12751 6
A Promise to Repay *Amanda Browning*	3477	0 263 12752 4
Happy Ending *Sandra Field*	3478	0 263 12753 2
An Unequal Partnership *Rosemary Gibson*	3479	0 263 12754 0
Angela's Affair *Vanessa Grant*	3480	0 263 12755 9
Windswept *Rosalie Henaghan*	3481	0 263 12756 7
Kiss and Say Goodbye *Stephanie Howard*	3482	0 263 12757 5
Shotgun Wedding *Charlotte Lamb*	3483	0 263 12758 3
Scandalous Seduction *Miranda Lee*	3484	0 263 12759 1
Tiger Moon *Kristy McCallum*	3485	0 263 12760 5
That Long-ago Summer *Sandra Marton*	3486	0 263 12761 3
Such Sweet Poison *Anne Mather*	3487	0 263 12762 1
Backlash *Elizabeth Oldfield*	3488	0 263 12763 X
The Price of Desire *Kate Proctor*	3489	0 263 12764 8
Perilous Refuge *Patricia Wilson*	3490	0 263 12765 6
Fully Involved *Rebecca Winters*	3491	0 263 12766 4

MASQUERADE *Historical*

Brighton Masquerade *Petra Nash*	M261	0 263 12862 8
Rebel by Moonlight *Elaine Reeve*	M262	0 263 12863 6

MEDICAL ROMANCE

Goodbye to Yesterday *Sarah Franklin*	D179	0 263 12868 7
Calling Nurse Hillier *Elizabeth Petty*	D180	0 263 12869 5

LARGE PRINT

A Summer Storm *Robyn Donald*	415	0 263 12593 9
Time to Let Go *Alison Fraser*	416	0 263 12594 7
The Wrong Kind of Man *Rosemary Hammond*	417	0 263 12595 5
A Kind of Madness *Penny Jordan*	418	0 263 12596 3
Lightning Strike *Marjorie Lewty*	419	0 263 12597 1
A Suitable Match *Betty Neels*	420	0 263 12598 X
Lovespell *Jennifer Taylor*	421	0 263 12599 8
Sicilian Vengeance *Sara Wood*	422	0 263 12600 5

Mills & Boon

MAY 1991 HARDBACK TITLES

ROMANCE

From the Highest Mountain *Jeanne Allan*	3492	0 263 12785 0
Spring Sunshine *Sally Cook*	3493	0 263 12786 9
Some Kind of Madness *Robyn Donald*	3494	0 263 12787 7
Nights of Desire *Natalie Fox*	3495	0 263 12788 5
Brazilian Enchantment *Catherine George*	3496	0 263 12789 3
After the Roses *Kay Gregory*	3497	0 263 12790 7
Dangerous Engagement *Lynn Jacobs*	3498	0 263 12791 5
A Forbidden Loving *Penny Jordan*	3499	0 263 12792 3
Dark Guardian *Rebecca King*	3500	0 263 12793 1
Yours and Mine *Debbie Macomber*	3501	0 263 12794 X
Romance of a Lifetime *Carole Mortimer*	3502	0 263 12795 8
The Most Marvellous Summer *Betty Neels*	3503	0 263 12796 6
A Fair Exchange *Valerie Parv*	3504	0 263 12797 4
Pink Champagne *Anne Weale*	3505	0 263 12798 2
Tattered Loving *Angela Wells*	3506	0 263 12799 0
Gypsy in the Night *Sophie Weston*	3507	0 263 12800 8

MASQUERADE *Historical*

The Devil's Bargain *Gail Mallin*	M263	0 263 12864 4
The Inherited Bride *Sarah Westleigh*	M264	0 263 12865 2

MEDICAL ROMANCE

Always on My Mind *Laura MacDonald*	D181	0 263 12870 9
Tansy's Children *Alice Grey*	D182	0 263 12871 7

LARGE PRINT

Rancher's Bride *Jeanne Allan*	423	0 263 12617 X
The Stefanos Marriage *Helen Bianchin*	424	0 263 12618 8
Something from the Heart *Amanda Browning*	425	0 263 12619 6
The Land of Maybe *Sandra Field*	426	0 263 12620 X
Mississippi Miss *Emma Goldrick*	427	0 263 12621 8
Jungle Lover *Sally Heywood*	428	0 263 12622 6
The Threat of Love *Charlotte Lamb*	429	0 263 12623 4
No Reprieve *Susan Napier*	430	0 263 12624 2